BREAKING WITHOUT YOU

A FRACTURED CONNECTIONS NOVEL

CARRIE ANN RYAN

Find your connection!,

Carrie Ann Ryan

Breaking Without You
A Fractured Connections Novel
By: Carrie Ann Ryan
© 2019 Carrie Ann Ryan
ISBN: 978-1-947007-43-7

Cover Art by Charity Hendry
Photograph by Sara Eirew

For more information, please join Carrie Ann Ryan's MAILING LIST.
To interact with Carrie Ann Ryan, you can join her FAN CLUB

PRAISE FOR CARRIE ANN RYAN....

"Carrie Ann Ryan knows how to pull your heartstrings and make your pulse pound! Her wonderful Redwood Pack series will draw you in and keep you reading long into the night. I can't wait to see what comes next with the new generation, the Talons. Keep them coming, Carrie Ann!" – Lara Adrian, New York Times bestselling author of CRAVE THE NIGHT

"Carrie Ann Ryan never fails to draw readers in with passion, raw sensuality, and characters that pop off the page. Any book by Carrie Ann is an absolute treat." – New York Times Bestselling Author J. Kenner

"With snarky humor, sizzling love scenes, and brilliant, imaginative worldbuilding, The Dante's Circle series reads as if Carrie Ann Ryan peeked at my personal wish list!" – NYT Bestselling Author, Larissa Ione

"Carrie Ann Ryan writes sexy shifters in a world full of

passionate happily-ever-afters." — *New York Times* Bestselling Author Vivian Arend

"Carrie Ann Ryan's books are wickedly funny and deliciously hot, with plenty of twists to keep you guessing. They'll keep you up all night!" USA Today Bestselling Author Cari Quinn

"Once again, Carrie Ann Ryan knocks the Dante's Circle series out of the park. The queen of hot, sexy, enthralling paranormal romance, Carrie Ann is an author not to miss!" *New York Times* bestselling Author Marie Harte

DEDICATION

To those who were left behind.
Like me.
Like my family.
Like so many others.

BREAKING WITHOUT YOU

From NYT bestselling author Carrie Ann Ryan, comes a brand new series where second chances don't come often, and overcoming an unexpected loss means breaking everything you knew.

I fell for Cameron Connolly at the wrong time. And when he left, I thought my life was over. But then, after the worst happened, I truly understood what that phrase meant. Now, he's not ready for a second chance, and I'm not offering one. Though given that our families have been forced together after losing one of our own, I know there's no turning back. Not this time. Not again. Not when it comes to Cameron.

I never wanted to hurt Violet Knight, but there were reasons I had to leave all those years ago—not that she'd believe me if I told her what they were. I not only left her, I also left my foster brothers. Honestly, I didn't want to come back to Denver to help run my father's failing brewery. But when it comes to my brothers, I know I'll find a way to make it work. Perhaps I'll even earn Violet's forgiveness and face the connection we both thought long forgotten in the process. Because I wanted her then, but now I know I need her. I just hope she needs me.

AUTHOR'S NOTE

I've suffered from depression and anxiety for over half of my life, perhaps longer at this point. I'm a survivor like many of my readers and friends. I lost two close friends to depression when they took their own lives. So, I have been on both ends of the pain that comes from this disease.

The Fractured Connections series is what happens after you lose someone. I've had the idea for this series for a couple of years now, but after I lost my husband suddenly to a brain bleed, I *needed* to write about what happened after. What happens when you have to live on without those you love.

Allison, a character you will not meet but who is on each page by just her memory, lost her battle with depression and anxiety. She was a fantastic person, one who smiled and held parties, who lifted up her friends and always had a joke for those who needed it.

Her suicide is not on-page, is not detailed, and is not glorified. I talked to other survivors, had them read this book as well as help me with certain scenes before I even wrote a word. But there still could be some difficult topics for some.

If you need help, please reach out to someone. We do not need to suffer in silence. We do not need to suffer alone.

PROLOGUE

I'LL ALWAYS REMEMBER.

They say that some points in time will stay with you no matter what happens. But they also say that you can ignore those times, that you can bury them and move on.

Those people don't know anything.

Because I'll always remember.

Of all the people who could have walked through that door, of the numerous individuals who had keys to that home, it had been me.

I was the one to see.

I was the one to find her.

And I'll always remember.

Because you never forget when you see the end.

Even when it's not yours.

CHAPTER ONE

Sometimes people just don't get it.

- Allison in a text to Violet

VIOLET

IT DIDN'T SEEM right that the sun was shining, and that birds were chirping in the air. It didn't seem appropriate that the sky was free of clouds, or that the world seemed to scream of beauty and peace.

I didn't find it fitting at all.

Because I was outside this afternoon instead of working or being with my family. I was watching strangers lower my best friend into the ground.

My best friend wasn't supposed to be dead. We weren't

even thirty yet. No, *I* wasn't even thirty yet. She would never reach it.

I watched as they lowered the casket inch by inch—ashes to ashes, dust to dust, as the saying goes. I watched it all and didn't shed a tear. I'd done my crying. I had lost so many tears, so much of myself with each crying jag and hiccupping sob.

I couldn't cry just then.

I was surrounded by my family, my friends, Allison's family, and everyone who had known my best friend throughout her life.

She had been such a joy, such a bright spot in this sometimes-dark world. She'd made me laugh, made me smile. And she had done so for countless others, as well. She was the happiness we all craved.

But all of it was a lie.

I knew that now. I'd discovered that the Allison I thought I knew hadn't been the Allison she'd hidden deep inside.

That shamed me. It made me want to leave, made me want to throw myself to the ground and curl up into a ball. It made me want to switch between pitching a fit and just weeping and praying that something could be changed.

It made me angry, it made me sad, but mostly...*mostly,* I just felt ashamed.

Because Allison was lying in that casket, wearing a blue dress that made her pretty blue eyes stand out.

No, that wasn't right either. Because Allison's pretty

blue eyes were closed, and they wouldn't be looking at anything anymore. No more searching for the next best thing, no more looking for anything.

Allison's parents had decided not to do organ donation, even though I knew that Allison had wanted to do it. She hadn't put it on her driver's license, though, and since we were not old enough in our minds to finish our wills, there hadn't been instructions for burying my best friend.

I was going to make a will as soon as I could. Because I did not want my friends mourning for me while wondering what I had wanted, and then watching it slip through their fingers when they realized that my parents were the ones in control.

Allison hadn't been married, hadn't had a power of attorney.

When she died, her parents had been the ones to make all the decisions, and that should have been fine. But I knew Allison—at least I thought I had. And so had my sister, Sienna, and our other best friend, Harmony.

The three of us thought we knew what Allison would have wanted.

We figured she would have wanted to be cremated, her ashes scattered to the wind in the different places that we had known and loved together. That was something I wanted, as well. I vividly remembered my conversation with Allison about it one night when we all got a little too drunk and started talking about death. It was something that a lot of people talked about, at least that's what I thought. It was part of everyone's future—the end, the idea that you wouldn't be around to make your own plans unless you wrote them down ahead of time.

But I didn't think that any of us had written them down. Well...maybe Harmony. Harmony had been through her own heartbreak. She probably had a full list of what she wanted when her end came.

But now, I was going to make sure that I had my list. Because Allison had not been cremated. Her organs had not been donated. She was going into a hole in the earth, and her parents had every right to make that decision.

I wasn't going to hold onto any bitterness when it came to that. I had enough for everything else that had happened. I didn't want to hold onto that and only remember watching my best friend being lowered into the ground and the darkness that came with that.

Hell, I didn't want to remember any of this at all.

But it wasn't like I had a choice. This day would be in my memory until the day *I* died. Until somebody tossed my ashes to the wind.

I closed my eyes and held back a groan. *No, Violet, it will be before that, won't it?* Before ashes and dust. I honestly wasn't really thinking clearly.

I almost jumped when Sienna reached out and squeezed my hand. My little sister—not quite so little since we were both nearly thirty—leaned into me, resting her head on my shoulder.

We were almost the same height, but I was wearing

taller heels, and that meant she could easily place her head on my shoulder. I wanted to turn around and just pull her into my arms, tell her that everything would be okay. And knowing Sienna, she wished she could do the same for me.

I tore my gaze away from the hole in the ground where Allison lay and would forever stay until she was no more, dust to dust and all of that. When I turned, my gaze met Harmony's where she stood stoically on the other side of Sienna.

Harmony had her dark red hair pulled back into a bun, and I didn't really understand why she had done that. She usually wore it down. All of us generally had our hair in long waves or straightened. The four of us had decided to see who could grow their hair the longest and the fastest. Harmony had won, but for some reason, her hair was back today.

Then I remembered.

It was how she had worn her hair at her husband's funeral.

She hadn't wanted to look the same as she had every day when she had known and loved her husband. She'd wanted to appear different than when he had seen her, the times when he had played with her hair with his fingers.

So, she had worn it back.

It seemed we each had a special way to wear our hair, our makeup, and ourselves for funerals.

I wasn't even thirty yet, but I had been to enough funerals for a lifetime.

I didn't want to go to any more.

I didn't want to be here at Allison's. She shouldn't be dead. She had been alive and healthy and whole just a few days ago. But now I knew that maybe she hadn't been. Perhaps she hadn't been healthy or whole at all.

Maybe that's why she'd ended her life at the age of twenty-seven. Just a year younger than me.

The four of us had been friends since high school, Sienna and I being close for far longer since we were sisters. We were all in the same two grades and became fast friends. We had even gone to the same college, and all stayed in Denver to retain our friendship.

I knew that not everybody had that ability. With the way everybody kept moving for their careers and the way the world seemed to become a smaller place, most people didn't have their childhood friends in their lives. But I was lucky. I had been able to keep my three best friends by my side throughout my pain—and theirs. We had grown together, lived together.

But now, there was only three.

We had lost our fourth.

And I didn't know what the next step was.

Whispers brought me out of my thoughts, and I tried not to feel selfish. I was so busy worrying about myself and how I was going to feel that I couldn't really think about the world without Allison in it.

Every single person around me had been connected to her.

My brother, Mace, was here, standing right behind me with his fiancée, Adrienne, at his side. He hadn't brought their little girl Daisy with them, as they hadn't known how she would react at a funeral, being so young. I understood that, though Daisy had known Allison.

I had been in the room when Mace explained to his daughter that Allison wouldn't be able to come back for another tea party. That she wasn't going to attend another Thanksgiving like she had the past couple of years.

I didn't cry as I remembered these things, although my eyes did burn.

Why couldn't I cry? I should be crying.

Sienna was crying. Harmony was crying. Adrienne was crying.

My mom was sniffling on Mace's other side, my dad putting his arm around her shoulders as he held her close. I had witnessed that as I turned to look before, but I knew he would still be there, comforting her.

My parents were sweet, amazing, and they had loved Allison like their own daughter.

And now, Allison wouldn't be coming home.

She wouldn't be doing anything.

Allison's parents stood on the other side of the casket, crying into their handkerchiefs. They were poised, prim, and a little separate from the rest of the world. They had been that way long before they heard that their daughter wasn't going to wake up again. I remembered going over to spend the night at Allison's house when we were in high school. Her parents were nice but very reserved. Though that didn't mean they were bad parents. They were wonderful, and Allison had loved them. I just didn't think they had known their daughter as well as maybe my parents knew me.

But, then again, I hadn't known Allison the way I probably should have either.

Maybe I would have seen it if I had. Maybe I would have been able to stop it. Or, maybe, I was being selfish again and just needed to stop and breathe.

Others began talking, and I knew we would soon be moving from the cemetery to the wake at Allison's parent's home. They had a large house that could hold everybody so we could eat, drink, and maybe laugh at some memories.

I didn't know if I could do any of that, though.

I had only been to one funeral before—Harmony's husband, Moyer.

I didn't even know if I remembered that as clearly as I should. And I never asked Harmony if she did. I always felt like I shouldn't. There were some things you just didn't talk about until the time was right. I just didn't know when that time would be.

My gaze traveled over the rest of the mourners, and then I sucked in a breath.

I should have known they would be here.

Of course, they would be here.

The Connolly brothers had known Allison almost as well as the Knight siblings and Harmony did. Even if they hadn't been in our lives for a few years, the Connolly brothers had been part of our crew when we were in college and were very much part of Allison's life back in high school.

I let out a shaky breath, willing the guys not to look up and meet my eyes. I knew I shouldn't study them, shouldn't look at them. But I hadn't seen them in so long, even though I knew they had moved back to Denver.

Everybody in our circle had known.

There was Brendon, the eldest, and the one in a neatly cut suit. I knew he grieved. He had been friends with Allison just like his brothers. But I didn't really know him all that well. I didn't know how he felt, but I was glad he was here just the same.

Because that meant Allison wasn't alone.

None of us were.

Next to Brendon stood Aiden, his hair a little messy, grief clear on his face.

I finally felt a tear fall and quickly wiped it away as Sienna squeezed my hand, letting out a sob of her own.

Aiden and Allison had been *the* couple in high school and into college. They had eventually broken up, not because they hated each other, but because they hadn't been right for each other. That was what Allison had always told me anyway, and I believed it. Aiden had moved on, maybe not to other women, but to other parts of his life. I knew he had gone to culinary school and was a chef somewhere now, but I hadn't really heard much about him since he and Allison broke up.

But now he was here, watching the first love of his life fade away into the darkness.

Another boy was standing on his other side, an older teenager. He had the look of the Connollys, but I had never seen him before.

After the Connollys' father had passed away, I hadn't known there were more foster brothers added to the family. The other three had been adopted in high school, though Aiden and his twin, Cameron, were biological brothers, as well. Maybe the boy I didn't recognize wasn't a brother at all. Perhaps he was just a friend. And maybe it was none of my business since I had no idea what they were all up to these days.

My gaze traveled to the right of the young man, and my jaw tightened.

The final brother.

Cameron. *That* Cameron.

The one that had broken my heart and walked away as if he hadn't known that he held it at all. He still looked as sexy as ever with his dark hair brushed back from his face and his beard just past scruff. Today, he wore a suit just like his brothers, but I had never known Cameron to live in one like Brendon did. Even Aiden wore suits more than Cameron.

Cameron was rough. Edgy. Dangerous.

He was a man that I hated, the first man I had ever loved, the first for a lot of things. And he was *here*. In my presence. I wasn't going to be selfish and make this all about me, but I hated that he was here. I didn't like that I had to see him today of all days.

But I would push that thought out of my head because today was not about me. It was all about Allison. Today was about my best friend.

I pulled my gaze away from the Connollys and focused on what came next. We made our way to the cars and then to Allison's parents' house. All the while, a drum beat behind my eyes started, telling me that a migraine was coming on. I quickly popped a pill and then chugged the water that Sienna handed over to me without asking. I knew that I would be incapacitated later, but maybe it was something I deserved.

I hadn't had a migraine in over two weeks, but this one was coming for me soon. That much I knew. Though with everything that had happened, I was surprised that it hadn't come on sooner.

It was going to hurt, but maybe I needed that pain.

We walked through the halls of the home that Allison had grown up in, the house we had all slept in a time or two. We had gotten ready for our junior prom here, although my sister had been in the grade below us and was only allowed to attend because she was going with a junior boy. Somehow, we had made it work so we could go to almost every dance together, even when we left Sienna behind in high school.

Today I walked through these halls again, looking at the photos of a young Allison on the walls.

My fingers traced the edge of one of the frames, and I let out a deep breath.

Everything was going to be okay. Because it had to be. Life would move on. It always did.

I just didn't want it to move on without my best friend.

I walked to where the food was, where everybody was gathered and talking. It wasn't that the whispers had gotten any louder, but maybe it was just that I was finally listening.

"I heard she took pills," a voice said from far off in the distance.

"Yes, then drowned herself in the bathtub," another voice said, equally as vicious but still almost sickly sweet.

"You know, I heard the police found no note. They don't know how she did it. We don't know exactly how she did it. And nobody knows why. Maybe her friends do."

I ignored that last voice, or at least I tried to.

Then there was another.

"You know, it does seem out of the blue. But maybe if we keep looking, we'll see what happened. I mean, no one just does this."

I swallowed hard and then took a few steps away. My hands were shaking, and I tried not to listen to any more of the murmurs.

Of course, there would be speculation. Of course, there would be whispers. Allison was bright and cheery and far more energetic than any of them or us.

Gossip had run rampant when Harmony's young husband died, but we had pulled through. We stood together as a team, the four of us, and made sure that Harmony knew that she was never alone.

And I was going to do the same thing now. So, I took a few steps towards Sienna and Harmony. The three of us grabbed hands, standing in a circle that was one shy of what it used to be. It was odd. I could actually feel the distance between us growing because there wasn't that fourth person in the circle, clasping hands as we always had.

The actual physical representation of what we were now hit me a little too hard, and I blinked quickly. I had only shed that single tear, and I knew I couldn't do any more.

Not with all the eyes watching me. Not with all the whispers.

Mace and Adrienne had gone home, not being able to stay for the wake because they still had to drive over an hour back to Daisy. My parents had gone as well, my father battling a cold. He would be fine, but I knew that the day had taken a lot out of him.

All of them would have stayed for me and Sienna and Harmony if we needed it.

But we had each other.

We had each other.

"They're all talking about it," Sienna murmured.

"Just ignore it. It's always best just to ignore it." Harmony's voice was a little shaky, but she held her chin high.

"I hate it. I just want it to go away. I just want to go sit up in Allison's old room and play a stupid board game like we used to." I closed my eyes, the headache starting to push its way into my brain. I knew it would likely transform into something more soon, the lights getting a little too bright, the tastes in my mouth going bitter.

"We need to get you home soon," Sienna said. "I can tell a migraine is coming on."

"Yes, it's going to suck. Let's just stay for Allison's parents for a little longer, see if there's anything we can do for them. Then, I'll go home and lick my wounds."

"I love you guys," Harmony said, bringing both Sienna and me in for a hug. So I leaned on my friend and held my sister close. This wasn't right. It wasn't supposed to be just the three of us. I mean, I knew that it would be eventually, but when we were older—far older when we were watching over our grandchildren, maybe even our great-grandchildren if things worked out.

We weren't supposed to be doing this at such a young age.

It wasn't fair.

But, as they say, life isn't fair.

Death shouldn't be either.

Allison's mom called out for Harmony, and she squeezed my hand before walking off to join the other woman. One of the caterers needed help with something, and Sienna charged in to assist, not even bothering to see if anyone else would offer to help. That was my sister. Always there.

That was my friends, we were always there for each other. Even if not all of us were here anymore.

The headache was coming on strong, and my hands had started to shake. I knew I needed to leave soon. The others would understand if I left, even if I had been the one to say that I needed to stay. Because I knew that I wouldn't be able to drive home soon if I didn't go now. So, I went over to the coats, slid mine on, and ignored more of the whispers as people tried to catch my eye. They wanted to talk to the girl who had found Allison.

I knew that much. But I had talked to the police, I had discussed things with Allison's parents. I had shared with my friends. I had talked to everybody about what I had seen, detailing it so much that I knew I could probably say the words by rote without even showing a single emotion.

Maybe that was for the best.

Because I didn't want to feel anything.

Didn't know if I really could.

So, as I turned away from the whispers and the knowing looks, I told myself that I needed to go home. Of course, just as I thought that, I slammed into a large chest.

A hard, *familiar* chest.

Of course.

"Violet," Cameron whispered, his voice rough, that low, deep growl that I remembered vividly.

"I—" I couldn't finish the sentence.

Because as soon as he wrapped his arms around me, the

dam broke. Tears slid from my eyes, and I let out a low groan that I knew others might hear. Cameron surely did.

In response, he let out a low curse that vibrated through my body and held me close. And I broke.

The others might not be able to see me, but Cameron could. And, of all the people I could have broken in front of, of all the individuals that could have held me when I shattered into a thousand pieces, it just had to be him.

He was the one who was there for me when I fractured.

Of course, he was.

CHAPTER TWO

CAMERON

I HAD EXPECTED some reaction the first time I truly saw Violet at the funeral, the first time that I spoke to her in what seemed like forever. I didn't expect the reaction I got. My arms were around her, holding her close as she quietly wept against my chest. I hated when she cried. I'd hated it when we were younger, and I damned well sure hated it now.

It didn't matter that we were at a funeral and crying was sort of expected, I didn't like to see her with tears in her eyes. I sure as hell didn't like it when those tears seeped through the shirt of my suit. It all felt too real, and I didn't want to feel anything real just then.

"Come with me," I whispered, pulling her towards the other end of the hallway.

There was nobody near, but I knew that other people

could probably hear. Violet was being pretty quiet, and I was doing my best to do the same, but some people probably knew that she was crying—on my chest. And the fact that they were already gossiping about numerous other things having to do with Allison meant that they would easily add something else to talk about.

When people were hurting, when they were at a loss for what to do, they sometimes just talked. I understood that. Didn't mean I liked it.

I tugged Violet, lightly so she wouldn't think I was manhandling her, and she thankfully started to move. Of course, if needed, I probably would've forcefully hustled her into another room just so she could breathe. Yes, I was an asshole, but it was for good reason.

At least that's what I told myself sometimes.

"You can let it all out. I'm here." I knew it was the wrong thing to say as soon as I said it. She froze in my arms, so I closed the door behind us and gave her some space. She took a step back, blinking wildly.

Her mascara and eyeliner had run down her cheeks, her nose was red, her face was splotchy. Violet had never been a pretty crier. That was something we both knew. Not that what I thought about her really meant anything anymore. After all, I had left. It didn't matter that I'd had a good reason. I took off without a fucking word. So, I probably deserved the anger in her eyes now, and the fact that her hands were fisted by her sides. I probably deserved all of that and more.

If her brother were here, Mace probably would've kicked my ass. Not only because of what I did in the past but because she'd been crying in my arms. Mace would've likely thought it was my fault.

Because it was always my fault, it seemed. Though I deserved that.

"I...I didn't realize you were right there. I'm sorry for bumping into you. Thanks for getting me out of view of everyone else." Her voice was cold, even though there was a bit of scratchiness to it that told me her crying was far from over.

"I just happened to be the guy you ran into. Is there anything I can do?" She shook her head and wiped her face, looking as put-together and sexy as she always did. Damn sexy. She had been stunning and gorgeous when we were younger. Now, she was a fucking bombshell. It was really hard to remember that we were no longer a couple. And we wouldn't ever be again. That was my fault, though. I knew that.

Violet shook her head and pinched the bridge of her nose. It looked as if she might have a headache, but I couldn't be sure. "I made a scene. I hate making scenes."

"You didn't make a scene."

She rolled her eyes, finally looking more like herself than the red-eyed, crying girl that she had been just moments before. "Of course, I did. They all heard. They've been talking shit about Allison already. And probably about me, too. But I'm done. I need to go. Thank you for being there.

Of course, it was you who was there. Of course, it had to be you, Cameron."

I didn't know why, but as soon as she said my name, I straightened, swallowing hard. She'd said my name countless ways before, sometimes in anger, sometimes in lust, sometimes just with happiness.

But, hearing it right then, I knew that I had missed it. Oh, I had known long before this, but with Violet right in front of me, it was easy to remember what life was like with her in it.

And that was a damned shame because, from the look in her eyes, this was as close as we would ever get. But that's all I wanted anyway. I had enough going on around me. I didn't need to deal with Violet Knight and everything that we had dealt with in the past.

"Do you need me to find your sister?"

"I'm fine. Just fine. Go back to your brothers. Go back to your brewery. Just go back to the life that you so desperately craved. Because you're not in mine, Cameron. I hope you remember that."

And then she walked out, slamming the door behind her. Okay, it wasn't quite a slam because she obviously didn't want to make a scene, but it was close. My head hurt. I was such a damned idiot. But I always had been, so there was nothing new about that.

I followed Violet out of the room, wincing when I realized that we'd actually gone into the guest bedroom where people would have gotten the wrong idea if they'd seen us.

Because they always jumped to conclusions when it came to us. Really, everything about me. Nobody trusted the Connolly brothers. They never had. And they probably never would. It didn't matter that all of us had our own businesses, or at least we had at one point. It didn't matter that we had all made something of ourselves and weren't the same kids and teenagers we were when we first moved into the area.

No, back then, we were just three kids who had been forced into a new family. We were just kids from the wrong side of the tracks. And it didn't matter that most of us had money now, we were still trying to figure out how to leave a legacy that wasn't ours to give.

And now I was thinking way too hard about something that really had nothing to do with me anymore.

Because while I might be back in Denver, it didn't mean I'd be back forever.

Well, maybe I would be. I didn't really know, and that was probably why I had a headache. That and the fact that I had just watched a girl I'd known, one that had fallen in love with my twin brother back in high school, being lowered into the ground. She was dead, and I didn't even remember the last thing I'd said to her. It wasn't like she and I were friends, at least not recently. We hadn't really seen each other at all since I walked out of Violet's life—and out of my brothers' lives for that matter.

I'd seen Allison once or twice, maybe at the grocery store or the bar. But we hadn't really spoken. I hadn't been her friend over the past few years. But she hadn't been mine either.

I didn't know why I felt shame crawling up my neck at that or when I thought about the fact that I hadn't really thought about Allison much at all since I left. I had enough crap to deal with. I also had much more on my mind than I once had.

My brothers were waiting by the door for me, giving me odd looks. When Aiden handed my coat to me, I shoved it on. We said our goodbyes and paid our respects to Allison's family before jumping into Brendon's SUV.

Brendon had driven because he was more of a control freak than the rest of us. Not that that was saying much since we were all a bit controlling. It just hadn't made sense to take more than one car when we were all coming from and going back to the same place.

Aiden sat in front with Brendon, not even looking at me. My own twin brother, my flesh and blood, not even giving a damn. Maybe he cared too much, and it hurt to look. It was hard to confront a person that was your mirror-image and yet not know them at all.

We'd been close as hell when we were really young. And then we'd been pulled apart because the system hadn't worked well enough to get both of us in one place. I hadn't seen my twin for years, hadn't known if he was okay, hadn't even been able to write.

It wasn't as if they gave foster kids the addresses of

where their relatives went. It didn't matter that Aiden and I were twins, they'd split us up anyway.

It wasn't until Jack and Rose Connolly came into our lives that Aiden had come back into mine. Jack and Rose, yes, just like the couple from *Titanic*. They had adopted three boys all at once. We'd started off as fosters, but then we'd taken their name. Brendon was the oldest, though not by much. And then came me, and then Aiden. I remembered joking that I was the older twin, therefore, the wisest one.

Yet I was the one who'd made the stupidest mistakes when we were younger, so maybe Aiden was the wise one.

We were brothers, the three fosters of the Connollys who'd become the three Connolly brothers.

We'd been everything to each other, and then Rose passed away, and things didn't seem as important anymore. Rose died, and some part of Jack faded with her. She was the only mother I'd ever known—in reality anyway. Oh, I remembered my birth mother, had seen her more than a few times, even after the adoption. But she didn't have custody of us, had lost it because she preferred the needle or whatever she could stuff up her nose to the two twin boys that she had given birth to. Oh, yeah, Aiden and I came from great stock, products of a junkie and some John who knocked her up. It was something the kids on the playground always liked to make fun of us for.

Snapping myself back to the present, I realized that I wasn't alone in the backseat. It wasn't something I could ignore, at least not over the past seven years. Or rather, *he* wasn't something I could ignore.

Dillon sat beside me, scowling at his phone as he played some game where he tried to milk cows or something. Yes, the eighteen-year-old who thought he was a master guitar player and who was now currently still staying with me because of obstacles out of my control was playing a farm game. Yes, it was one that I played when I was bored, but I wasn't going to really think about that right then.

"Did you finish your chores?" I asked, nudging Dillon with my arm.

I didn't fail to notice that Aiden stiffened in his seat, and Brendon's hand tightened on the wheel.

Dillon was the elephant in the room, the eighteen-year-old that hadn't been a surprise to me but was a surprise to them.

Yes, I was an asshole.

But when your drug-addled mother comes to you and says she needs your help—and you go—you have to deal with the consequences. Aiden hadn't gone. He hadn't wanted anything to do with our birth mother. And I understood that. Even if I was pissed off at him and hated myself because I hated *him* sometimes, I got it. Our mother was a bitch, a liar, and a thief. I didn't ever want to call her a whore, but others did.

She had never been a good person. She had beat us, used us, and probably would have tried to sell us one day if she could.

But she had needed help with another son.

Dillon.

My brother. *Aiden's* brother.

And while not by blood, maybe Brendon's brother, too.

And so, the elephant in the room, the boy who thought he was a man, currently sitting beside me. He looked up and nodded, even as his eyes narrowed, and he glared.

He was such a little asshole sometimes, but then again, so was I. And I didn't have the excuse of being a teenager.

"I did. I wanted to get it done before we went. I didn't know Allison, but she seemed like a nice lady from what others said. I'm sorry she's gone."

And that was why I liked this kid. Maybe I even loved him, but I'd done a really good job of burying all of my emotions and feelings for the past seven years. But Dillon was good. Even if we'd both fucked up with the whole college thing.

I wasn't a dad, I'd never claimed to be, but I had failed when it came to Dillon. And he had failed himself, as well. The little shit had lied about planning for college, about submitting his applications and wanting to do everything himself.

Instead, he had decided to move to LA, even though we were on the outskirts of it anyway when we lived in California. No, Dillon wanted to be the next big rock star in the greatest rock band of his generation. Though it wasn't like I actually knew the names of current music groups anymore, so I couldn't even say where Dillon got his influences.

Then my kid brother's little friends had decided that they were going to college because their parents had actually forced them to do their applications. Maybe if I had done the same, Dillon wouldn't be forced to take a gap year. Or, perhaps, if Dillon hadn't been a little liar, he wouldn't be in the situation he was.

"Allison's a great woman," Aiden said, his voice gruff. Dillon met my gaze, and I gave him a slight nod. Aiden coughed. "*Was* a great woman."

Aiden didn't speak to Dillon often, and I didn't blame him for that.

When I went out to California to check on our mom, I'd found this kid—a boy who wasn't quite as little as I thought. An eleven-year-old full of temper and hatred. So, I moved there to try and help. I'd tried to get in contact with Aiden during that time, attempted to tell him that we had a brother.

But Aiden didn't accept a single call. Not for a year.

And I'd stopped trying.

Because I had chosen our mother over Aiden—at least that's how he saw it. So, I guess I deserved the fact that Aiden hated me.

But Dillon didn't deserve it. And so, the family drama that was the Connolly family was never-ending. Because Jack died too, damn it. Old Jack died and left the family business to us.

A failing brewery that brought the Connolly brothers back together.

And while Dillon might not be a Connolly, at least not in name and even though Jack and Rose had never met him, he was my brother. And I would just have to reconcile the fact that things were different now. And that I had no idea how to clean it up.

We pulled up behind the brewery, and I winced at the fact that there were still a few spots open. It was early evening, it should be the start to the rush. There should be more cars in the parking lot. When we walked in, I held back another curse. There sure as hell should be more people sitting and having a brew. It was right about the time of the evening that the early people would come in for their beers. At least that's how it'd always been for Jack and Rose.

But not anymore.

The place wasn't actually a brewery anymore, it was a bar. It'd used to run craft brews before craft beer was a thing and I came into the family. The bar, however, had kept the name and the label, still selling their microbrews as well as some crafts and domestics that were the mainstay of most bars.

The four of us went to the back, Dillon having already taken off his tie, Aiden and I pulling at ours. Corporate Brendon kept his on as if he'd been born in a suit. It was kind of funny considering that, as a kid, he'd never worn a suit and sometimes didn't even wear two shoes. But I knew that Brendon sure as hell had a lot of shoes now.

"So, what are we going to do now?" Brendon asked, sitting on one of the chairs in the private, back room.

Aiden flipped the chair around and sat in it backwards before speaking. "Well, if we're going to finally fucking talk, I guess we should try and fix this place. Because we can't let Jack and Rose's place go. The Connolly Brewery has always been part of this neighborhood. We're not going to lose it."

I narrowed my eyes. "You say the 'neighborhood' as if it isn't downtown Denver. Breweries come and go." I knew that better than my brothers did since I'd owned my own with a partner back in California.

"Shut the fuck up, Cameron."

Dillon's wide gaze moved from me to Aiden and then to Brendon before going back to his game. Dillon was here because I was his guardian. It didn't matter that the kid was eighteen now and didn't technically *need* a guardian. He lived with me, and I wasn't about to let him go home alone where I couldn't watch him. So, that meant Dillon was part of these family discussions. Because, damn it, Dillon was my family. I'd just have to figure out how to put all of the rest of it back together again.

"The bar is failing, it's in the red, and we're going to have to change that. I know the three of us moved back because Jack asked us to in the will, and so we're here, but it's been a few months now, and we haven't done anything. We'll have to start doing it. Cameron, I know that you sold your half of the brewery back in California to move out here, so what are you going to do now?"

"What I've been doing. Working behind the bar." I'd moved back after Jack's death, and I'd done my best to keep the bar running since. Then Brendon returned. It had taken him a little longer to wrap up everything with his personal life.

Aiden had just arrived, finally leaving the restaurant he so desperately craved to be a part of. I didn't know the story behind it and, damn it, I wished I did. Because that would mean Aiden was actually fucking talking to me.

"There needs to be some changes," Brendon said quietly. "We can't keep it open like this."

"Just shut up," I said, running my hand through my hair. "Just...not now. Not the day we buried Allison."

Aiden narrowed his eyes. "Really? You're going to be the one to bring her up?"

"Because you haven't yet. But I know it's on your mind. Let's just take today. We just need today."

"You're the one who said that when we lost Jack. You're the one who said we needed that day, needed some time. Well, enough time has passed." Brendon stood up, shaking his head. "And, you're right, I'll give you today. But, tomorrow? Tomorrow, we're going to figure out what the fuck we're doing. Because tomorrow might be the beginning of the end when it comes to this place. And I don't want that to happen. You may think I do because I wear a suit and I have a different job than you. But I love this place. It's our home. And we left that. We left Jack behind. So, now, we have to fix it."

Brendon stormed out, and Aiden left right on his tail. I looked over at Dillon, who was doing his best to just stare at his phone. There weren't any games on it this time. Just a blank screen.

"Let's go home."

"It's weird calling it *home*. We're not even out of boxes yet."

"You're right, kid. I guess we should fix that."

"I'm not a kid."

I shrugged. "Jack always called me 'kid.' Even when I was in college." I winced, but Dillon didn't say anything. I probably shouldn't bring up the college thing, but now that it was out there, I continued. "We'll get on that, too. We'll get on everything. I guess our time of mourning Jack and what we all had is over. Probably has been since we walked into the place. You know? We'll get it done. We have to."

And I knew we would.

I'd save the brewery.

I'd save Dillon.

As thoughts of Violet's wide eyes brimming with tears filled my mind, I hesitated. It wasn't my place to save her, but maybe if I weren't such an idiot, I could fix what I broke there, as well.

Maybe it was time. Maybe it was past time.

CHAPTER THREE

People are the worst. But you're still my person
- Allison in a text to Violet

VIOLET

I LOVED MY JOB. I truly did. But on days where all I had was headaches, false starts, and the inability to focus, I didn't know if I actually liked it.

No, that wasn't really the case. I just didn't like my life at the moment. I didn't hate my job, I just really hated this day.

I was exhausted, mostly because I hadn't slept the night

before and because it took so much extra energy to remain happy and appear whole these days. My brain still ached just thinking about Allison and everything that had come with that. My heart hurt, my body hurt...everything hurt just thinking about my best friend.

Coming home after crying on Cameron's shoulder, or rather his entire chest hadn't helped things. I came home after practically running from him and had fallen into my migraine spiral. I was used to them, and they came often. No amount of hormones or Botox or drugs could help my migraines. They were just a part of me and something that even my boss knew about. Thankfully, his wife suffered from debilitating migraines as well, so he understood, and we worked around my illness when it came to my job. I wasn't really sure how it would have worked if he weren't so accommodating. What wasn't helpful was the fact that not everybody understood my migraines, and some—mostly the woman who sometimes shared my lab bench—thought me being home and having extra time was because of something else.

She thought the fact that I sometimes needed to stay at home, trying not to throw up all day because I couldn't see straight, had to do with her. Yes, I came in and worked on weekends. I worked long hours when needed. I got my work done, no matter the cost or the time.

But Lynn *always* thought it was about her. After all, we had been friends for a few years before we ended up not being friends anymore. But it wasn't really my fault. She was currently married to my ex-husband and had been with him before he was my ex.

Yes, I had somehow become a cliché. I'd married someone who I thought was a decent guy, a man I thought I loved. And maybe I *did* love him. But he didn't love me the way he should. We were married for eight months. Eight freaking months where I'd thought I was doing okay. But everything had changed over a year ago. Everything fell apart.

Kent Broadway had cheated on me. I should have known a man named Kent would do something like that. I tried to go with the whole Superman/Clark Kent thing, but, every Kent in every book and TV show I'd ever seen or read other than Superman was an asshole. Maybe there were good Kents in the world, but not mine. I know I shouldn't call him *my Kent*. There was nothing *my* about that Kent.

So now, Kent and Lynn were together. Married. And good for them. Because I didn't have to think about him anymore. Ever.

Okay, I had to think about him every day I was at work because I was an environmental chemist and worked my ass off alongside another in the field. Lynn.

I had been the one to introduce Kent and Lynn, and they'd hit it off. I'd been so happy that my work friend and my husband were friendly. Because that didn't always work out. I really hadn't been friends with any of Kent's coworkers or their wives. We just hadn't meshed. But that was fine. You were allowed not to get along with everybody in your life. But, apparently, the two people I intro-duced had gotten along a little too well. And that made me a little sick. I hated the idea that I had to work alongside the woman who'd taken the man I didn't even love anymore. I wasn't even sure I ever truly loved Kent. And maybe that was on me. But, mostly, it was just the whole situation. It made me feel weird and like I was messing things up.

But I was getting used to it. Kent and Lynn had been married a month, and Lynn was finally back to work after her long honeymoon and vacation. The two of them had taken a three-week trip all over Europe. While there, she had posted all sorts of photos on social media, and even though she had unfriended me, our mutual coworkers were constantly commenting on the pictures. Therefore, I saw them. It wasn't like I tried to run away from it, but it was hard to pretend that I was okay. I really wasn't anymore. Everything was falling apart around me, and yet it had nothing to do with Lynn or Kent.

That was in the past. I had been divorced for a year now, and that really wasn't what was on my mind.

No, what was constantly on my mind was the fact that Allison was dead, and there was nothing I could do about it. And the fact that I had felt more of a connection with Cameron after I yelled at and cried on him than I had ever felt with Kent.

And what did that say about me?

How self-centered was I, that those were the two things

on my mind? And not because of what they were, but because of how they revolved around me.

Why didn't I see that Allison needed help? Why couldn't I see that she was drowning?

Why couldn't I foresee that she wasn't going to be here anymore because of something inside of her? I hadn't seen any of that. What did that say about me?

No, it wasn't truly about me, but maybe I'd been selfish enough that I missed the warning signs. Or maybe there hadn't been any warning signs at all, and I was just reaching for answers to something I couldn't change.

And then, added to all of that, I was worried that Kent had cheated on me because it was my fault.

God, there was something truly wrong with me today if that was where my mind had gone.

Because it didn't matter that I'd had a connection with Cameron when we were younger. It didn't matter that I had loved him with all my heart. I had fallen out of love with him when he broke me into a million pieces. When he shattered me like glass against stone.

I was dust in the wind when it came to my relationship with Cameron. It didn't matter that he was still sexy as hell and had no right to be. It didn't matter that I still felt that little pulse inside my gut when he held me. It didn't matter at all.

Because I was not with him, and I was never going to *be* with him. He didn't fucking matter.

Yes, I had loved Kent. No, I wasn't in love with him, and

yes, I had fallen *out* of love with him faster than I had with Cameron, but maybe that was for a reason. People loved others differently. Every relationship was different. Maybe I had the most the first time, so I wasn't going to hurt as much the second time. Or maybe I was just tired and needed to stop whining to myself. It was stupid.

I was feeling stupid.

"Violet, darling? Is everything okay?"

That set my teeth on edge. *Darling.* Lynn calling me darling. She hadn't called me that when we were just friends before she became a two-timing tramp.

Oh, God, why did I think that?

It didn't matter that she had cheated. It didn't matter that she had helped my husband commit adultery. I should not call her a tramp. Calling other women names was wrong.

And yet, I still hated her.

Even if I didn't want to. Even if I didn't really feel that deep of an emotion and was more just *blah* when it came to Lynn. I honestly didn't really feel anything about her. Maybe I should be more ragey. Or perhaps I was losing my freaking mind.

"What was that?"

I tried not to say her name, mostly because when I did, she gave me this sad, puppy-dog look like she was worried about me. Why should she be worried? She was the one who had to sleep with Kent for the rest of her life. She was the one who would have to go down on him because that's how he liked to orgasm. He never liked to come during intercourse.

Oh, God, why was I thinking about things like that? Bile rose in my mouth, and I tried to shake away the horrific thoughts. Maybe I needed to have sex again.

It had been over a year, after all. Maybe sex would help things. Or perhaps drinking. Wine would help. Yes, wine.

I didn't have a migraine, wine would definitely help.

"I just wanted to make sure that you were doing okay. You've been staring off into the distance rather than at your paperwork for a while. I did want to say that Kent and I are so sorry about your friend, Allison. The few times that we met her, she seemed so nice."

We. All of those we's. Kent had known Allison better than Lynn because I was married to the man. But as was the way with overlapping friendships, she had known Allison, as well. But they hadn't come to the funeral, and for that, I was grateful. Not because it had to be about me, but because I didn't want it to be about me. I hadn't wanted the additional whispers about the girl who had found Allison dealing with the fact that her ex-husband and his new wife were there.

It was all so exhausting—putting all these labels on everything. It just made me tired.

And it made me realize that I was once again staring off into the distance, and Lynn was giving me that sad, puppy-dog look that I hated.

"I'm just thinking, no worries about me."

"Well, if there's anything I can do, just know that I'm

here." She squeezed my shoulder again and smiled at me. I ignored the touch.

I just nodded, giving her a smile. See? Everything was okay. Or it would be. I was a professional, and I got my work done, even if my brain sometimes decided to go off on a tangent. No, it wasn't easy working with the woman my ex-husband had married, but it wasn't the end of the world either. I had seen the equivalent of that. I had watched that end happen as they lowered Allison into the ground. Working with Lynn seemed like a small drop in the bucket.

That oddly calmed me.

So, I rolled my shoulders back and went back to looking at my data as Lynn walked back to her own paperwork, texting as she did. No doubt messaging Kent, but that was fine with me. I honestly didn't care.

Truly.

I was an environmental chemist who worked at the University of Colorado at Denver. I was listed as an associate professor on the tenure track, but I wasn't actually teaching this year. They'd dropped one of the classes that I normally taught, so now I just put in more hours in the lab. I worked under one of the tenured professors, but I had my own research team of grad students and undergrads that wanted to follow the grad-student track.

I really loved what I did, even if it stressed me out sometimes. Lynn worked under the same professor, but she was actually teaching two classes this year—one with the undergrads, and one of the small set of grad students we actually got at the university. We weren't the main University of Colorado campus, but we were growing bigger on the Auraria campus each year. As soon as they built the new science building and added more dorm rooms downtown, everything had changed just a little. It was far different than it was when I had gone here.

I hadn't actually decided to come back and work here until the position opened up and one of the professors that I'd had when I was an undergrad offered me the job.

I didn't make beaucoup money, but I didn't need to. I got to study the ways the city of Denver and its suburbs affected the environment. Because we were surrounded by mountains and lush greens, yet we were still in a desert period. I enjoyed going down to Cherry Creek and running samples, then going up into the mountains to take samples there. It just depended on what area of study I was focusing on for the semester. There was just so much to the way Colorado's environment impacted the city and vice versa. It made for a rich study.

It would be easier if I could actually get more funding, though.

I snorted, shaking my head. Since I wasn't teaching this semester, I was on a federal grant, which was actually harder to come by these days than it had ever been before. And with the way things were turning out, I was afraid that it would be impossible come next year. A lot of my friends were having to either work on new areas of study or get second jobs not focused on research.

Things were shifting dramatically, and I knew that I couldn't just keep my head down and focus on my work. Not entirely. I had to be aware that, one day, I might not be able to do the research I was doing, despite the fact that it was desperately needed with the way our environment and climate were changing.

But, right then, my focus had to be on the numbers in front of me. It was all about pH and other data for now.

The information I worked with today would help me tomorrow, and maybe help someone else a few years from now.

See? I loved what I did. Even if the lack of funding, the fact that I worked with my ex-husband's current wife, and my migraines that came out of nowhere, sometimes made me not want to work at all. But I really liked shoes, and I liked a roof over my head. And, occasionally, I actually liked a good meal that wasn't frozen or a can of green beans.

My stomach rumbled at that thought, and I snorted. Apparently, it was lunchtime, even though I should probably keep working. So, I noted the time and worked for another twenty minutes, making sure I stopped at a place I could come back to later. Then I locked up all my stuff and went down to the break room to eat my lunch. We were chemists, so it wasn't like I could just eat at my desk. My work area was surrounded by things I really didn't want my food near or vice versa. I really didn't want chemicals in my food as it was.

Then again, my brother was a tattoo artist, and I knew

he didn't work while he was eating either. Yes, he may be able to have a drink when I couldn't, but he still didn't eat a sandwich with one hand as he tattooed someone with the other. The thought actually made me smile.

I sat in the break room, looking out the window towards the mountains. Today was a pretty clear day, and I was grateful for that. We'd had a few horrible fires during fire season, and the haze from that had been ridiculous. When the rain finally came, it had cast a pall over the Rockies so even though the smoke was finally gone, there were so many clouds it was hard to see the mountains at all. It wasn't until recently that I had been home one day as the sun was setting and I could see the sun from behind the mountains, turning them a dark purple. The effect was so vivid, I knew that I would actually be able to see the mountains the next day.

Now, I looked out at what I studied, what I loved. With my job, there were a few places that I could live, but this was the best for me. This was what called to me. This was my home. My parents lived here, and the rest of my family. Yes, Mace was about an hour south, but I saw him often. Even more so now that we were making sure we didn't lose touch.

I loved Denver. It was a part of me. I would never leave my friends or my family.

I looked down at my packaged salad and frowned.

Allison had left us. She had left, and I didn't know why.

It was the idea that I had to come to terms with that, which scared me more than it probably should.

I was a scientist. I needed answers. And there weren't going to be any of those for me. Not for any of us.

I let out a shuddering breath and wiped at a tear, grateful that there was no one else in the room. Sienna, Harmony, and I would have to go through Allison's things soon, something that her parents had asked us to do.

Although they had taken care of all the funeral arrangements and made decisions that I might not have agreed with at the time but understood, they were letting us deal with her apartment and her things. I wasn't sure that they would have been able to do it themselves. And, one day soon, I would be grateful for that. But right now, the idea of going through things with Harmony and Sienna hurt me. It was like a sharp, stabbing pain that ebbed to a constant, dull ache.

But I would do it because it's what Allison deserved. I missed her with every breath, but I couldn't bring her back just by missing her.

I couldn't do a lot of things.

For some reason, the memory of Cameron holding me when I broke filled my mind again.

I knew that I would be forever grateful that he had been there to keep me away from prying eyes, but I truly wished it hadn't been him.

Because he'd brought back all sorts of feelings.

So many memories and emotions that I shouldn't feel.

My life wasn't as complicated as I was making it seem, at least to myself. But right then, with everything going on, I sometimes wished I could just go back to the way things were in college. When there was laughter before there was heartbreak. Before there had been loss.

But there was no going back to that.

This was my life now.

And if losing Allison had taught me anything, it was that I would have to learn to live it.

Even if it hurt.

CHAPTER FOUR

CAMERON

I WORKED AT A BAR, needed a damn drink, and wasn't going to get one anytime soon. I should be used to it by now though, because I didn't really get what I wanted often.

And that made me sound like a petulant child, but sitting here listening to my brothers who didn't really feel like brothers anymore, trying to change everything that had once brought us together didn't make me feel like I was winning.

But maybe there was no winning in this. Maybe there couldn't *be* any winning in this.

"There needs to be more changes, Cameron." Brendon paced the office floor, pinching the bridge of his nose. He had been sitting behind the desk at first, pouring over accounts and paperwork. The ledgers might be mostly electronic, but my brother had wanted to look at all of them in hard copy again so he could focus. That meant they appeared to be piled almost to the ceiling at this point. The fact that my brother was probably the best tech wiz out of all of us was a non sequitur. Brendon just needed something tactile when he was stressed.

I was also stressed out, and that meant *I* needed a damn drink. "I know we need to make changes, but that doesn't mean we have to change *everything*. Next, you'll want to take down that prop from *Titanic* and remove everything that was Jack and Rose."

Above the arch to the hallway that led to the restrooms was an old, carved, wooden sign that said, *I'll never let you go...unless you need to.* I loved that damn sign.

Aiden let out a grunt and shook his head. I glared at my twin. "You have something to say?"

"You know, I think you're saying enough for both of us, don't you?"

"Stop it," Brendon snapped. "We don't have time for bickering."

"We always have time for bickering," I said casually. "It's what we're good at."

"Now you're just being a dick," Brendon said, looking down at his papers again.

"Why don't you say that to my face, asshole?" I stood up, clenching a hand into a fist. I needed to punch something. Needed to do anything but sit here and listen as everything changed, while I felt completely out of sorts. I wasn't an idiot. I knew that we needed to do some things to help the business. But going in and changing the entire menu, the atmosphere, and most of the things that were done for years seemed like a lot all at once.

And maybe it was because I was stressed out about Dillon and my own life, but the fact that I was back here at all when I didn't know if I would ever come back didn't help.

But it didn't matter.

Nothing mattered.

And maybe that was the problem.

Brendon looked up then and clenched his jaw before he spoke. "Stop it. Just stop it. We're not going to fight. We're not going to act like we're teenagers again. You came here knowing that there would be some changes. You came here with Dillon for us to figure out what we needed to do next. We don't want to lose the bar. Hell, I know it sucked when the brewery shut down, and we weren't even here then. We're not going to lose this part, Jack's legacy. But we're going to have to make some changes. Something you damn well know. We're in the red. Jack was in the red for long enough that we may lose the place unless we get some steady business."

"I know all of that. I looked over the numbers just like you did. I'm the one who used to run bars and breweries in California."

"I know. That's why I'm so confused that you're pressing back so hard."

I sighed into my hands and then ran my fingers through my hair. "I know it doesn't make any sense, and I *know* that I'm being unreasonable about some things. But can't we just go slow?"

"We can go slow and still change the food options. We don't need to have the same bar food that's on all the menus around us that nobody wants to eat anymore since they're clearly not doing it here. People are only coming in for the beer, which is great. But we make more money with food." Aiden folded his arms over his chest and glared at me. My twin was really good at that, but I couldn't really fight back. I had moved away, and Aiden hadn't followed.

Maybe we needed to deal with that, too. Just not now.

"But what are you going to do? Make something pretentious and froufrou?"

Aiden flipped me off. I kind of deserved it, I was being an asshole. "Shut the fuck up. I left my job at a Michelin-starred restaurant to come work at a pub. So, yeah, I'm going to implement some changes. I'm going to add tapas and different things that will make us stand out. You can fight all you want, but that kitchen is mine. So, you better back the fuck off."

Aiden stood up then. Looked like I might be getting my fight, after all.

Brendon stood in between us, shaking his head. "I can't right now. I seriously cannot with the two of you. Yes, Aiden, we are going to use some of your new food. But you aren't going to take away all of the bar food. Because we are a bar and grill."

"We don't actually have *grill* in the name," I said, knowing that both of my brothers would glare at me.

Aiden turned, his hands on his hips. "I'm not going to take away your precious wings or anything like that, but I'm going to add some things. We are in foodie nation. People like to try new things. We can have the normal fare, and then we can have a dash of something different. Let me do what I need to do in my kitchen. I'm good at my job. There's a reason I was the top sous chef at my restaurant."

I didn't add that my brother never would have made it to the head chef position because the owner of the restaurant had let his son take the job. Aiden wouldn't have made it to the next step in his career because the new head chef and the owner would have made it impossible for him. I didn't know everything that had gone on, but I knew enough. Aiden might have left everything behind when he came back to work at Jack's place, but he also needed a new start. We all did.

"I have a few other ideas, but I need to work them out before I bring them to the table." Brendon played with the cuffs on his shirt, rolling them up on his forearms. The man always wore a button-down, even when he was in jeans and trying to be casual. I never really understood it, but I knew it's what made my brother feel comfortable, so whatever.

"Fine. Do what you want. I'm going back to the bar to

help Beckham because I know we're going to get our one rush of the day soon."

"We'll have more rushes." Brendon sounded so earnest, I wanted to believe him. I truly didn't want to think about the fact that this could be the last few months that we worked at this place. Maybe it would have been easier to shut it all down and start over somewhere else, but that was only in the numbers. That didn't take into account the memories, or the sweat and tears. This was Jack and Rose's place. We weren't going to fuck it up.

Apparently, we *were* going to change it.

"I'm heading back to the kitchen to see what I can do. I don't want to change everything, Cameron." Aiden glanced at me then, and I froze. He looked so honest, so much like me when I was lost. It startled me sometimes to remember that we were twins. We had been best friends, brothers by blood, and foster brothers. And then we walked away from each other.

It was hard coming back, but it was even harder to face the fact that I had left at all.

"Just don't add an *amuse-bouche* or something that takes dry ice or requires changing states of matter."

Aiden snorted. "Molecular gastronomy is not my favorite thing. I know it works in some restaurants, but I've always been more of a meat and potatoes guy."

That made us all laugh, considering that Aiden had tried to be a vegetarian at one point for Allison, though neither of them had ended up remaining so for longer than a month. Aiden might like meat and potatoes, but he also made it fancy as fuck. That's what made my brother so good at what he did. But that didn't mean I had to enjoy all the changes coming at me. And maybe it was because I was feeling a little lost about not being able to help Dillon and being back in town with all of these memories slammed into me, but it all made me feel on edge. Or maybe it was the fact that I kept thinking about Violet and how she'd felt against me when I held her.

Damn it, I really needed to stop thinking about Violet.

"Seriously, though, I'm going to work at the bar. Let me know if you need me."

"Is Dillon busing tables?" Brendon asked, his voice deceptively calm.

"He is. He's not old enough to work behind the bar yet, but he can bus tables and, eventually, if he's not a brat, he can be a waiter."

"And is that what he wants to do? Be a waiter?" Aiden asked, his voice emotionless. Damn it. I needed to figure out what to do about Aiden and Dillon since I wasn't sure the two had actually spoken a complete sentence to each other, but tonight wasn't that time.

"No, he wanted to be in the next big band. But that didn't work out all that well. So, we're working on figuring out college forms. And don't even get me started on the student aid. FASFA is the devil."

Brendon snorted. "It really is." He paused and then looked up at me. "If, uh, you need help with that, let me know. Numbers are sort of my thing. And I'm pretty good at paperwork." He held out his hands, gesturing at the papers on the desk. I nodded, a lump in my throat.

"I might take you up on that. I mean, I'm good with the paperwork for the bar, but going to college was not really my thing. At least the paperwork wasn't."

Aiden sighed. "We all went to college, but I think Jack and Rose took care of all the paperwork for us."

"And I will always be grateful for that," I said, laughing. "I know Dillon and I are working on what college he needs to go to. We'll figure it out."

Aiden stuffed his hands into his pockets and rocked back on his heels. "You know, I hear Violet works at UCD. I mean, she's pretty close to here and probably knows all about colleges."

"Don't go there," I said, shaking my head. "We can't go there."

"Sometimes, I don't think we have a choice." Brendon said the words softly, not looking at either of us.

No, sometimes we didn't have a choice in what happened around us. But, sometimes, we needed to make that choice for ourselves.

I gave each of them a nod and went down to the bar where, thankfully, a nice, late-evening rush was coming in. I had opened, and I would probably end up closing with Beckham. We couldn't afford more than the two of us as bartenders right now, but both of us needed the work. Beckham was about my age, had a big beard, and long hair tied behind his head. He looked almost hipster, but I had a feeling he had been like that even before it was a thing.

That thought made me laugh, and Beckham raised a brow. "What's so funny?" he asked, his voice low. Beckham rarely smiled, and he didn't laugh. At least not since I'd known him.

Jack had hired him on when we were all out of town living our own lives. Beckham and some of the waitstaff were the only ones that stayed on after Jack's death. It made sense to me. Food service wasn't an industry where everyone stayed at the same job for years. We could pay them, so that wasn't the issue. It was more that they hadn't wanted to work with anyone but Jack, or they had moved on because it was their time.

Now, we had new staff in the kitchen—people that Aiden was dealing with, thankfully, not me. And we had a few new waitresses. And one new busboy.

Dillon.

"I'm just thinking about stupid shit," I said quickly, finally answering Beckham's question. "What can I do to help?"

Beckham just shrugged, pulling two drafts before going down to get a couple more mugs. "I'm filling up some pints for the guys at the end. I think Tracy's going to come by with an order for some mixed drinks, though." He tilted his head towards the redheaded waitress who was at a table with five women. "Pretty sure they're not the beer type."

I narrowed my eyes at the group of ladies and nodded.

They were all dressed to the nines and giggling. Probably starting their evening before they did a Denver bar crawl. "That happen often? People coming in here dressed to the nines?" I'd been working here for a couple of months but still hadn't gotten used to the clientele since I was usually in the back—or had been before Brendon came to work here full-time on top of his other job.

Beckham just shrugged, sliding the beers down the bar into the waiting hands of the men at the end. Then he went back to pulling more drafts, not even looking at what he was doing. He just knew where everything was. He had been doing it for years, apparently.

"Not often. We have a decent happy hour on vodka, so sometimes people start here, mainly because they came here to eat lunch with their parents or something and know the place. It's familiar. The girl in the black, the one with all the sequins or whatever glitter crap that is? Her dad comes here often. So, it's not like we're a big place that college girls come to for drinks. But we do okay. People like us. They remember us. It's just making sure that new people can find us, I guess."

I blinked, wondering where all the words had come from. Beckham didn't speak often, but when he did, what he did say seemed to be important.

Beckham had been right, Tracy slid over five orders of various vodka drinks that would be a pain in the ass to make. But I didn't mind. This was my job, after all. I might like owning businesses, but I also liked working with my hands and mixing drinks. There was chemistry to it, making sure that everything was just right. Because when you worked with fresh ingredients, the recipe wasn't exactly perfect. You had to alter it depending on what you were using. That's what I liked. So, I went back to work, quickly mixing the five drinks. Dillon came by to help as a barback.

"Anything else?" Dillon asked, glaring. I knew my little brother didn't like working behind the bar cleaning up, and he sure as hell didn't like busing tables. But Dillon needed a job, and I needed the help. The kid got paid, and I could also keep an eye on him.

"We're good back here. But it's getting busier, so I guess you working over in that section is probably good."

"Is Brian coming in tonight?" Dillon asked, mentioning the other busser we had.

"No, you're by yourself here. Do you think you can handle it?"

Dillon just snorted. "I think I can handle busing a few tables. It's not brain surgery."

"Is that what you want to do? Be a brain surgeon?" I didn't know what Dillon wanted to do with his life, but then again, I didn't think Dillon knew either. I also didn't think that at eighteen you could really make decisions about what you wanted to be when you grew up. You were still growing up, so taking some gen-ed classes and figuring out what your major could be, seemed like the best course of action. The whole idea that you had to figure out your entire life at age fifteen while you picked out where you wanted to go to college seemed ridiculous. Not that I actually told Dillon any of this because I was still pissed off that he had lied to me.

And I was still mad at myself that I hadn't noticed.

"I don't want to be a brain surgeon. I don't really like blood," Dillon said, and I laughed.

"I'm not a huge fan of blood either. We shouldn't be talking about blood and other bodily functions while we're working anyway."

"True. Okay, I'm off to go clean up after those guys. I think they threw half their wing bones on the floor."

"Damn. Do you need some help?" While Dillon needed to work, and I needed to make sure that he was keeping on the right track, I didn't want him cleaning up after assholes.

"I said, I have it." Then he stomped off, and I just shook my head, watching him go. Beckham gave me a look that I couldn't read, and we both went back to work.

A couple of hours later, I felt the hairs on the back of my neck stand up.

I knew it was her before I heard her voice.

Violet was here. And so were the others.

I hadn't known that they came to this bar. I hadn't seen them since I came back to town, but here they were, in my place.

"I got this," I said to Beckham as I went over to where Violet, Sienna, and Harmony were sitting.

"Hey." I stuffed my hands into my pockets, wondering if I could be more of an idiot. Probably.

"Hi," Sienna said, kind of smiling. The expression didn't really reach her eyes, but I didn't blame her. Everything was still so raw and emotional for them. Violet's little sister felt things strongly. She always had, even when we were younger. I didn't know how she felt about Allison. I didn't know how any of them were feeling. Hell, I didn't know how *I* was feeling about Allison.

But I was glad that they were here, even if it confused me.

"It's good to see you, Cameron," Harmony said softly. She grinned, but like Sienna, it didn't reach her eyes. Damn it. I wished I could help these three, but I was already out of my depth with so many other things, this would just make it worse for everyone.

I looked over at Violet, clearing my throat. "Can I get you ladies something to drink? To eat?"

"We're here to make sure that the Connolly brothers know that we're supporting the bar," Sienna said when Violet didn't reply.

I turned to Violet's sister. "Really?"

"Of course. We've come in on and off over the years, but it's been more off since we've been so busy with our lives. But that's going to change. We need a new place to actually sit and drink that's not our house with a bottle of wine. Because while that's good, sometimes, you just need to get out. So you're stuck with us. And we need booze. We need lots of fucking booze."

Her eyes filled, and Harmony reached out and grabbed her friend's hand. I cleared my throat and nodded.

"So, what are we having?"

"Beer and shots," Violet said.

My brows rose. "Really?"

"Do you think we can't handle it?"

I met Violet's gaze and shook my head. "I think you can handle just about anything, Violet." I regretted the words as soon as they left my lips. "I know what you guys like. I'll be right back."

Then I walked away, wondering if I really knew anything at all.

Because, right now, it felt like I *was* nothing.

CHAPTER FIVE

That's next level hotness right there

- *Allison in a text to Violet about George Clooney*

VIOLET

I WATCHED Cameron walk back to the bar and wondered what the hell I was doing. There were many ways to be a masochist, but apparently, watching my ex-boyfriend walk away while we were in his family establishment was a new way to have it happen. Maybe I liked pain, perhaps I enjoyed that burning sensation around my heart that had nothing to do with heartburn or any actual vascular disease, and everything to do with the fact that I was an idiot.

"The more you watch him, the more I'm afraid that we made the wrong choice." Harmony leaned forward and gripped my hand.

She was always doing that, making sure Sienna and I knew that we were loved and taken care of. I hated the fact that Harmony was actually getting used to the idea that this was her lot in life now. Apparently, one of my best friends in the entire world thought it was her job to make sure others knew that they were loved and cared for when the rest of the world was burning down around them. I hated it so much for her, but I didn't know how to make it better. I didn't know how to make anything better. I knew the three of us really needed to talk, we needed to make sure that not only were we there for each other but were also open about talking about Allison. I just didn't know when that time would come. Because it sure as hell wasn't now.

"I love this place." I shook my head as I squeezed Harmony's hand back and looked over at Sienna so my sister knew that I was telling the truth. "I really do love this place. Yes, it holds a lot of memories, and the current bartender who's not the sexy, bearded Beckham currently makes me want to pull out my hair, but that doesn't mean that I don't love this place."

For some reason, that sentence made Harmony and Sienna both laugh.

"What?" I asked, frowning.

"You just called Beckham sexy?" Sienna asked, looking over at the man who wasn't really our friend, mostly because we didn't know him all that well. But he was someone that I considered a pleasant acquaintance.

"Is he not?"

"Oh, he's sexy as hell. But I didn't think you would actually say that when there's another bartender at the bar that I would assume you would think is sexier."

"We are not going to compare bartenders. Plus, Beckham has this whole I-have-secrets-and-I'm-not-going-to-tell-you vibe."

"Oh, he totally has secrets, but don't you think Cameron does, too?" Sienna asked, giving me a weird look.

"Let's get off this subject, shall we?" I asked, keeping my voice pleasant. I felt anything but congenial just then, but it was my fault for coming here and daring to call someone sexy. Just because I thought Beckham was hot didn't mean I didn't think Cameron was sexy, too.

"Before he comes back, quick question," Sienna said quickly. "I never asked, did you ever find Aiden sexy? Because if you find Cameron sexy, then his twin has to be sexy too, right?"

There was something in my sister's eyes when she said that, and it kind of worried me, but now we were going way off track from any conversation that I wanted to have right then, and it wasn't like I could really figure out what was going on.

"Of course. But I was never truly attracted to Aiden the

way I was to Cameron. I don't know why. But you know they are different people. Hell, I used to think Brendon was sexy, too."

Harmony snorted. "Oh, I used to think Brendon was cute, as well. Moyer told him once, I think. Mostly because he knew it would make me blush."

I smiled. "I forgot that the two of them used to work together. "As soon as I said the words, I wanted to take them back. Because the reason that Harmony knew Brendon as well as she did was because Brendon used to work with Moyer, Harmony's late-husband. Everything was so convoluted and connected that it sometimes hurt to think about it. Especially because it wasn't supposed to be like this. I wasn't supposed to lose so much all at once. And Harmony sure as hell wasn't supposed to lose everything either.

"So, what do you think he's really bringing us?" Harmony asked, thankfully moving on and away from the subject of Brendon and any other conversation that could be awkward. Of course, everything that we were talking about today would likely be strange. We were sitting in my ex-boyfriend's bar, a place he owned now with at least his twin, someone who happened to be the love of Allison's life at one point. And the other brother in the place was a former friend of Harmony's late-husband. To say that everything was awkward would be an understatement. Of course, it was all strange. Because that was how we lived now. This was our life. Thankfully, before I could put my foot in my mouth again or wonder what the hell we were all going to talk about, Cameron showed up with a tray of pints of beer and six shots.

"Now, this is good Irish whiskey, but I'm going to hope that you all took a car service here. Because, if not, you're not getting a shot." He held up the tray and did indeed hold them back from us.

"Of course, we took a car service here. We want to get drunk. Being drunk is helpful."

Sienna smiled, and I wished I could be happy like that. I would have loved to act like everything was okay, as if I didn't feel like I was dying inside. It was all just too much. Being here with my friends and trying to act like we weren't missing our fourth, being here where I knew we would end up seeing Cameron, it was just hard. But I had put it out of my mind because we were trying to support the family who had always supported us. Jack and Rose had been part of our lives ever since we met the Connolly brothers. They had been an amazing couple who had taken on three foster brothers and brought them back together. They had even made sure to put Cameron and Aiden in the same home because they knew that the twins had been split up when they were younger.

When Cameron and I were dating, we had talked about how he felt about that, at least in a sense. We'd never gotten too deep, never dove beneath the fragile surface that was his pain. I had understood at the time that it would take longer. And I loved him. So, I would have waited.

But that time never came. Cameron had walked away.

"Well, now I can give you your shots."

"Well, we were going to pay for them anyway," I said and then groaned. "Never mind, ignore I said that. Of course, you're going to make sure we're not going to be drunk and getting behind the wheel. It's been a long day."

It had been a long week. A long month. But I had a feeling Cameron knew that.

"Of course, I'm going to make sure you guys are okay. I'm not going to let you guys get hurt."

I knew he hadn't meant to say that because his jaw suddenly went tight, and my belly clenched. Harmony and Sienna looked between us, slowly moving their beers and shots towards them as Cameron set them on the table. Nobody was talking. It had been awkward before, but now it was even worse. I swear I could feel every single eye on me like their literal eyeballs were sliming down my body as I tried to figure out what to say next. Why was I so awkward? Why was this so awkward? Why was my life so awkward?

"Do you want me to start a tab for you guys? Or is this going to be all for the table?"

Sienna was the one who answered. "Just a normal tab for the table. You might want to send out some wings or whatever Aiden's making, though."

"I'm sure Aiden will make you something fancy." Cameron didn't sound like he was too happy about that, and it had me wondering if Cameron liked any of the changes that I knew were probably coming to the pub.

I knew the bar was in trouble, only I didn't know exactly

what was going on. But the fact that all three brothers were back in town trying to take care of it meant that something else was going on. Aiden was like a Michelin-star chef or something close to that, and that meant that he probably wouldn't be happy making bar food all the time. I knew that Brendon worked with fancy companies and dealt in all the money—not that I actually knew anything about that since I made barely any money in my job. I might like shoes, but I also liked them gently used.

"How about wings and something that Aiden wants to make for the table." Harmony said it with a smile, but I still watched as Cameron's jaw clenched once again.

"I'll let him know you're out here." Cameron glared over at the teenager I'd seen at the funeral. "Hey, what are you doing?"

The boy looked up guiltily from his phone that he had pulled out of his apron pocket. "Nothing."

"What did I say about your phone?"

Cameron grumbled something under his breath and then nodded at the table before going off to join whoever that was. His brother? No, I knew all the Connolly brothers. Maybe his son? I froze at that thought. No, that wasn't possible. That kid had to be in his late teens. There was no way that he was Cameron's son. He did look like he was related to him, though.

"Who is that?" I asked, my voice low, not wanting others outside of our table to overhear.

Sienna leaned closer. "Dillon? I think Aiden said that's

their brother. I don't know the story, he sort of mumbled it to me when I saw him at the funeral, and I asked point-blank. Like I said, I don't know the story behind it, but he looks an awful lot like Aiden and Cameron. And because he didn't live here with Jack and Rose, he's not a foster brother. I know it seemed to hurt Aiden to even talk about it, though, so I didn't ask any more questions."

I sat back in my chair, blinking. Another brother?

That was different, but it was all a little too much for me to think about just then. I'd figure out what it all meant later. For now, I held up my shot towards the other ladies, who did the same. We clinked glasses, slugged them back, and then slammed the glasses on the table.

We each chugged half of our beers and then did the other shots before finishing the other half of our ales like we were younger than we were.

My stomach grumbled, and I knew that drinking on an empty stomach was probably stupid, but we were here to not only support the bar and the Connollys but also make the plans that we needed to for the next time we met up.

We needed to clean out Allison's apartment, and we needed to go through every single one of her things. And it was going to kill me, day by day.

No, I couldn't say that phrase. I couldn't say "kill me," or "I just want to die." All of those phrases that we use in the vernacular. Like "I could just kill myself" or stupid things like that. Because those were real words. And they really meant something.

Death was real. Allison was gone. And I needed to not be an idiot and use words that hurt, even if I was only saying them to myself. Cameron came over with a plate of wings and three glasses of water, as well as three more beers. He held back the shots, and for that I was grateful. Two shots and chugging a beer was probably too much for me already. I would likely feel it in the morning. But maybe I needed to feel it. Perhaps I just needed to feel period.

"Thanks," Harmony said as she handed out the plates that Cameron had given us. "They look great."

Cameron nodded. "We were always good with wings, Aiden makes the sauce even better. But don't tell him I said that."

"I heard you anyway," Aiden said, elbowing his brother out of the way. "Now, these are nachos, but not just any nachos. I added some shredded chicken and a little bit of better cheese than what you can squeeze out of a bottle."

He went on to explain the nachos in every single detail, and they did look fabulous. They may have sounded a little pretentious as he described them, but even then, the smell wafting up made my stomach grumble and my mouth salivate. Sienna was practically hanging off every word Aiden said, but then again, maybe I was just seeing things. Sienna and Aiden had always been friends, and we had hung out with Allison and Aiden often when they were dating. Or perhaps I was just trying to put a new spin on things so I wouldn't have to think about Cameron and the fact that he was still standing there, watching us.

"They smell amazing," I said as I reached for one. I took a bite and almost groaned aloud. It was only the fact that Cameron was still glaring that I didn't. Maybe if I really hated the fact that he was still there, I would have made more of a scene about it. But I didn't want to hurt him. The whole point of my pain was that I didn't want to hurt at all. So, lashing out wouldn't help. He had left years ago. I stayed. He hadn't given me a reasonable explanation, so I could be pissed at that. But I wasn't going to be petty and try to hurt him over nachos.

Delicious, amazing nachos. The best I'd ever had.

Oh my God, I wasn't going to make it much longer. I wanted to shove my face into the appetizer and eat them all.

Some look must have crossed my face because Cameron just snorted. "Well, apparently, the nachos are a hit. Aiden, I guess you win."

Aiden just grinned. "Of course, I win. And this is just the start. Just wait until you see what I can do with mushrooms."

"Like deep-frying them?" Cameron asked, and I knew he was just fucking with his brother.

But Aiden fell for the bait because he narrowed his eyes and opened his mouth, probably to yell. But before that could happen, Brendon walked in, a smooth smile on his face.

Brendon was always smooth. Sometimes, I thought he was *too* smooth, but I had seen the rough edges and knew there was more beneath the surface. He slid between the twins and put his arms around their shoulders. "I see that we have special guests tonight."

"Yes, but your brothers seem to have already noticed." Harmony laughed as she said it, and Brendon rolled his eyes.

It was nice seeing Harmony laugh, I didn't see it often enough. I would have thought that seeing Brendon would hurt her because whenever *I* thought of him now, I always thought of Moyer. But that wasn't really how Harmony felt. And maybe that was good. Maybe it was good that she would be okay, and that she wasn't stressing out like I was. Or maybe I was just going crazy.

"Why don't you join us?" Sienna asked, gesturing to the larger table that we were at. The rush seemed to be over, and I held back a twinge that it seemed to be over quite quickly. But with the food I was tasting, I had a feeling that maybe the bar would do better soon, especially if this was one of the changes the brothers were making. I hoped it would turn around because I didn't want to lose Connollys.

The bar. Not just the Connollys. I had already lost them, right?

"I think that could be arranged," Brendon said, taking a chair beside Sienna. Aiden took the chair nearest him so he was sitting beside me. Cameron just shook his head. I tried not to feel disappointed. There was no reason to feel that way. I didn't know this Cameron, wasn't sure I even liked him. But I sure as hell didn't like the fact that he reminded me of all the pain he'd caused when he walked away.

"I need to make sure Beckham isn't alone up there. I know we're not too busy,"—he paused, and the brothers looked at each other before looking away—"but he needs to take his break soon. Let me know if you need anything, I'll be sure to send Dillon over."

And with that, he walked away, and I wondered what the hell I was going to do. Because Cameron Connolly wasn't supposed to be in my life. Not anymore.

Yes, I had walked into his damn bar, but that didn't mean that I really wanted him in my life. I didn't want to have these feelings where I wanted to make sure that he was okay and comfort him. I wasn't supposed to want any of that. But, apparently, I was losing my mind.

Aiden brought out another dish, this time with pork belly and some other sauces that I hadn't really heard of before. That second beer after those shots had really hit me, and now I was drinking water. I didn't want to get drunk, I just wanted to stop feeling.

It was nice catching up with the guys, finding out what they had been up to and what they were doing now. But in reality, I just wanted to know more about Cameron. Because I'd missed him. I couldn't lie to myself and say I didn't. Because I did. He made me happy. Or at least he *had*. And, yes, I was probably setting myself up for more heartbreak even having him in my life, though it wasn't like I wanted anything more than him serving me booze and talking to his brothers. But it would probably happen. It usually did.

Aiden and Brendon didn't really talk about Cameron or

Dillon, but they were the two giant gorillas in the room. It was evident that Dillon was related to them, at least to the twins, but Aiden didn't talk about him at all. Didn't even look at him. And I had no idea what that was about.

All I knew was that Cameron was apparently hurt, and my stupid, emotional soul wanted to reach out and make sure that he was okay.

Maybe I did need more beer.

"Yeah, we're thinking about doing it maybe tomorrow or the next day. We don't have as much time as we should because of her landlord, but we'll get it done." I pulled my thoughts from my self-pity and looked up as Harmony casually mentioned the fact that we needed to clean out Allison's apartment. Sienna wiped away a tear, and Aiden leaned closer to my sister and gripped her shoulder before quickly letting go. Sienna didn't move towards him, but then I wasn't sure if she had noticed the touch at all. She was closing in on herself, much like I did. We were far too alike sometimes.

"We can help if you want," Brendon said then cleared his throat. "I know I helped when, well...you know."

I had forgotten that. I hadn't been able to help Harmony as much as I wanted to when she had to clean out some of her house after Moyer's death. Harmony had decided to move to a smaller place after her husband died. The couple had bought a larger home because they had been planning on having a family, and I didn't think that Harmony had wanted to live there once her husband was gone.

I didn't blame her for moving, but I hadn't been able to help with the move as much as I wanted to. My grant had been up, and I had been working practically twenty-hour days trying to make sure that I still had a job and that those under me could keep their jobs, as well. I knew Harmony understood, but I had never forgiven myself. But, apparently, Brendon had been there for her. He had been friends with Moyer, so it made sense.

"You don't have to help," I said quickly. "I mean, we might need some help with the heavy lifting, and I know that my brother wanted to come up from the Springs, but I don't know if he'll be able to." Mace and Adrienne were working harder than ever because their shop had made the national news and they now had to turn clients away at this point. So, it wasn't like he could really take time away from his family to come and help me out. He would if I asked, but if others closer could help, maybe we should take them up on it.

"Of course, we'll help," Aiden said. "You just tell us when you need us, and we'll be there."

Something warmed inside me, and it felt weird. I knew that my friends and I weren't alone. We had each other. We'd always had each other. But with my family so far away —even if only an hour—sometimes, I felt like it was just the three of us. The three of us against the world—when it should have been four.

So, maybe having help even in the form of friends that I had thought long gone, maybe that was good for us.

"I think that's exactly what we need," Harmony said, nodding.

Cameron didn't come back to the table. Instead, he sent Beckham. I didn't know if that was about the brothers or me, or if maybe he really did have to deal with the broken tap that Beckham mentioned. It didn't really matter, though, because we were leaving. And Cameron wasn't mine. He hadn't been for a very long time.

I made sure that I picked up all my stuff, still a little buzzed even with all the water that I drank and food in my belly. We said goodbye to the others, promising that we'd let them know when we decided to clean Allison's place, and then we made our way to the car service area and then home.

As soon as I walked through my door, I locked it behind me then slid to the floor, tears sliding down my cheeks.

Everything hurt so much.

Allison was supposed to be out with us. She would have been the one to make us laugh and bring the boys over so we could get over whatever issues we might have had with them. She would have been the one to make everything okay. But she was gone.

And I was left behind.

And it just hurt.

I hoped it wouldn't always hurt. But I was afraid. I was so afraid that it would.

CHAPTER SIX

CAMERON

"HEY, bro, I think your girl left this."

I turned around at the sound of Dillon's voice and frowned. "My girl?"

Dillon rolled his eyes like the eighteen-year-old he was. At least that had gotten better over the past few years. When the little brat had been younger, the eye rolling had never ceased. Ever. It was like a constant state of eye rolling. I wasn't quite sure how Dillon had been able to see anything when he was doing that constantly. But then again, I was pretty much the same way when I was his age.

"Your girl, the one who came with her friends that you were talking to. She sat with her friends that Brendon and Aiden seemed to know. You know, the ones from the funeral?"

"I know who you're talking about, but why do you think she's my girl?" I didn't know why I was continuing this odd conversation, but for some reason, I wanted to know why Dillon thought that Violet was my girl. Because she was definitely not mine. Not anymore. The way she could barely look at me was proof of that.

"Brendon mentioned it." The fact that the kid was talking to Brendon at all was a good sign. If only he could do the same with Aiden. Dillon continued. "He said that you used to date or something. I don't know. But she was there, and you guys had this whole like explosive chemistry thing going on—not that I know anything about that," he added as he held up his hands in a surrendering gesture.

Apparently, I looked slightly menacing or something, but I couldn't really help it. I hated the fact that my brothers talked about me behind my back, but then again, I sort of did the same with them when I was worried. Brendon wasn't technically Dillon's brother, but of the two of them, at least between Brendon and Aiden, Brendon was getting closer to Dillon.

Aiden was keeping his distance, and I understood that, after all, there was a lot of baggage when it came to the three of us and how we were related.

"She's not my girl anymore."

"Because you left?" A pause. "You left her because of me, right?"

I pinched the bridge of my nose, not really wanting to have this conversation but knowing that this one—as well as many others—were long overdue. Thankfully, we were in the back where it was just the two of us and Beckham coming in and out so we wouldn't be overheard too much. Because I really didn't want to have this conversation while I was with the rest of the staff or any customers.

"We broke up because I was an idiot."

"You cheated?"

I shook my head. "No, nothing like that. But I like the fact that you think cheating makes you an idiot. Because... don't cheat. That makes you more than an idiot. It makes you worse than the scum that you find on the bottom of your shoe. Just make sure you remember that."

Dillon rolled his eyes again. "Of course. I'm not a dork."

"Okay, then."

"But you still didn't answer my question. What happened?"

I shook my head. "That's something I really need to talk with Violet about first." I let out a sigh. "But I'll never regret finding you. I'll never regret being your big brother and having you in my life. I hope you know that." I stuffed my hands into my pockets, and Dillon did the same. I didn't even think he realized he had done it, or that it mirrored my movement and said that we were related in more than just DNA.

"Yeah, well, I guess you don't suck."

"Thanks for that. But you really think this is her scarf?" I asked, holding the silky, blue thing up close to my face. I could smell her on it, that sweet scent that was just

Violet. Oh, I had seen her wearing it, and I knew it was hers. I just needed Dillon to say it too, just to make sure that I wasn't imagining things. Or seeing things that I wanted to be true.

"It's hers. So, do you want me to put it in the lost and found, or do you want to go to her house and give it to her? That way, it's that whole, 'hey, you left this. Here,' thing."

"Really? What kind of movies have you been watching? I thought they all had things blowing up, not those romantic comedies you seem to want me in."

Dillon just grinned. "I watch things. I know things."

"Yeah, you sure do know a lot. Now, go finish taking out the trash, and I'll figure out what to do with this scarf."

"Just don't be all gross with it and like, jerk off into it or something. Okay? Because she seemed like a really nice lady, and you doing that...kind of creepy."

I let out a groan and pinched the bridge of my nose. "I'm going to pretend you didn't just say that. Because that is disgusting. And if I ever hear you doing any of that, well, I really hope I never hear about it. But if I do, I'm going to kick your ass."

"That sounds like a plan. Because I'm not some creepy jerk. I just really hope you aren't either. Now, off to the dregs. Yay for taking out the trash."

Dillon grunted and growled and went back to his work. I just rolled my eyes much like my little brother had done earlier.

"I'm losing my damn mind." And the fact that I was

talking to myself just told me that I'd probably already lost it instead of just started to lose it.

I looked down at the blue scarf in my hand and squeezed it just a little bit so I could feel the softness between my fingers. I knew where Violet lived thanks to Brendon, who seemed to know everything. I wouldn't have to ask anyone or even look her up.

Knowing it was probably a bad idea, I told Beckham that I was heading out for the night, well aware that the other man would be able to easily close alone since it was his job, and got into my car. I was probably making a huge mistake, but then again, I made a lot of those. More so recently than ever before.

And I wanted to see her. I wanted to make sure that she was okay. Because I knew she really wasn't, not after losing Allison. Aiden wasn't okay, how could Violet be?

She lived in a small house in one of the suburban neighborhoods close to downtown Denver. I knew she worked at the old university that we had all gone to, but it was kind of nice seeing her in a house that she owned, being a grownup. I'd just recently bought a small house that I shared with Dillon. I guess signing the papers meant that I was staying, even more so than me trying to fit in at a pub that wasn't really mine. Or one that didn't feel like mine anyway. I had made good money when I was in California, and selling off my old place had made me even more. So, I could send Dillon to college and not even have to worry about saving for it. Because I already had. I just hadn't been paying close enough attention to make sure the kid actually got in. But that was changing. I wasn't going to remain the idiot I had been, thinking that we had it all figured out and handled.

And now I was just stalling. I pulled into the driveway since Violet was either not home at all, or her car was in the small, attached garage. I really hoped she was home. I didn't know what I was going to do once I saw her, but maybe it would come to me by the time I made it to the door.

I gathered up her scarf and wondered why I was here at all. Maybe I missed her. Or maybe I just needed to atone for my sins.

Because there was sure a hell of a lot of them.

I knocked on the door, not wanting to ring the doorbell in case she was asleep. Not that I thought she would be, but I wanted to give her the opportunity to ignore me. Because she was allowed to do that. She was allowed to forget that I even existed. I had been an asshole, I had left, and I deserved whatever came to me.

But all those thoughts fled as soon as Violet opened the door, and I saw her wide eyes filled with tears, her cheeks red from crying.

"What's wrong?" I asked, instinctively reaching forward before pulling my hand back. She wouldn't want me touching her, and I would do well to remember that.

"I just had a tough day. What are you doing here? Is everything okay?"

I shook my head before moving my hand forward so she could see her scarf. "Everything's fine. My brother just found your scarf, and I figured I'd bring it to you. And now that I'm here, I realize that this was actually a really stupid thing to do. You could've remembered your scarf at any point and come back for it. Or maybe this isn't even yours, and I should just be going now."

I took a step back, grateful that she didn't have stairs on her front porch, when she suddenly moved forward and took my hand. I froze, wondering when I would stop reacting this way every time we touched. We used to touch all the time, used to do more than that. Now, just the feel of her made everything seem different. It was as if I was coming home. Not that I was actually doing so.

"Thank you for bringing my scarf back. I didn't realize I even left it. I guess I'm not quite all there right now."

I handed over her scarf, reluctant to let it go, and then stood there with my hands once again in my pockets, rocking back on my heels. "I'm glad that Dillon found it."

"Oh, it was Dillon? You said your brother and I thought it was one of the other two. Not that Dillon isn't your brother...I'm just rambling now. Do you want to come in?" She paused as if she hadn't really meant to say that, and I was a little surprised she had. "If you want. You don't have to. I just...I was just sitting here awkwardly in the dark, crying. So, maybe I could use some company."

I nodded and then took a few steps in as she gestured for me to enter. I liked the inside of her house—the warm colors, and soothing tones. Her couch was big enough that I could probably lay on it and not have to scrunch up. And that was saying something since most couches these days seemed to be too small for any man my size.

Not that I was actually thinking of myself on her couch. Not at all.

"Can I get you something to drink?"

"No, I'm okay. But are you? Why were you crying?"

She turned on more lights so I could see more of her, and I noticed that her eyes were clearing up a bit, her cheeks not as red as they had been when she first opened the door. "I'm just thinking about Allison. And the fact that she wasn't out with us tonight. And that your brothers are going to come help us clean out her apartment. It just sucks. And I hate that there're no answers."

"I hate that there are no answers for you either. For any of us. I know Aiden loved her back in the day, and I figured that they were still in contact with one another, but that was a long time ago. I hadn't really seen her since I left." I held back a cringe, not meaning to bring that subject up.

"I assumed you didn't talk to a lot of people after you left," she said, a bit icily.

I deserved that.

"I should probably apologize. Probably should have done that a long time ago." My words were soft, but they still felt like barbs.

"Apologize for what? Walking away without saying goodbye? Or leaving the rest of your family in a lurch just like you left me?"

"I deserve that," I said, my voice rough.

"Yeah, but maybe I deserve something, too. Why did you leave, Cameron? I figure it had to do with Dillon now that I know a bit more, but that doesn't make any sense to me. Why couldn't you tell me? Why did you just walk away as if I was nothing?"

I swallowed hard, my hands clenched at my sides. "That couldn't be further from the truth. You meant everything to me."

"Don't lie to me. If I meant so much to you, you wouldn't have left like you did."

This wasn't how I had wanted this conversation to go. Hell, this wasn't how I wanted anything to go. I hadn't come here to talk about this, but it was time. Everything was past time.

"Seven years ago, my mom contacted me. Not Rose, the one who birthed Aiden and me and threw us out on the streets after she overdosed. Aiden and I are twins, the same birth mom, same birth father. And you know I don't know who my dad is." I didn't know why I was repeating the obvious, but I needed to collect my thoughts.

"I know," Violet said, her voice soft. We were standing in her living room, facing off with one another as if this had been waiting for us this entire time. And maybe it had. I should have told her this before. I shouldn't have hurt her like I did. But I was young, stupid, and didn't know what to do with my own emotions, let alone hers.

But that was all on me. And I knew it.

"Mom was doing drugs, and Aiden and I were the result

of one of her Johns. She needed money for the drugs she loved, and so she sold her body. And while I will never judge anyone for the choices they make if they want to be a sex worker, I will always judge my mother for making the choice so she could shoot up again. I will always judge her for taking Aiden and I with her down that rat hole."

"Cameron, you don't have to start there if you don't want to. You just have to tell me why you left, not how you came here in the first place."

"But I have to. You have to know why it's all connected. And why I'm such a fucking screw-up."

"You're not a screw-up. Yeah, you screwed up, but you're not one."

"I sure as hell feel like it sometimes. But, anyway, Aiden and I were finishing college, and Mom contacted me. She left us before because she OD'd. She almost died, and the state took her away. I was born and raised here in Colorado but in the system most of the time. And then Jack and Rose took me in, and then they found Aiden."

"I had forgotten that, the fact that you and Aiden didn't grow up together."

Thankfully, Violet sat down on the edge of the chair and let me do the same. My knees were weak just talking about this. I wasn't a big fan of it. But she needed to hear it all. And maybe I needed to say the words.

"After Mom OD'd the first time when we were really young, they put Aiden and me into the system. Brendon was in the system too at that point, but we didn't know each other then. We were all just young boys who were split up into homes because no one wanted to take two twin one-year-old boys that may or may not have learning disabilities since their mom was on drugs when we were born."

"That's just cruel," Violet said on a whisper.

"That's life. Nobody wants to adopt grown kids. They all want little babies, and they sure as hell don't want kids that may have to deal with withdrawal at some point in their lives. Not that I remember any of that. Anyway, Jack and Rose adopted both Aiden and me, making sure we were in the same home, and then they got Brendon. And that's when you met us. In high school and college. The seven of us were all a big unit."

"I know. I was part of it. That's why I don't really get why you just left like that."

"Because while we may have been a unit, and while I loved you—"

"Don't say that. Not now."

"But I did. I loved you."

"Not enough. Obviously."

I held back a wince, knowing I deserved it. "My mom called me, saying that she had OD'd again and needed my help. I hadn't planned on going down there until I thought she was really going to die. So I left, only for a weekend I thought, and found out she was going to lose custody of her other baby if she wasn't careful. That boy was Dillon. It was with a different John, and no, I don't know who Dillon's birth father is. I'm not sure she does. Regardless, even though I hated my mother, I didn't want her to die. I don't know what that says about me, but I just didn't want her to die. And I didn't want her to take Dillon down with her once I found out about him."

I looked up, and Violet was wiping away tears, but I continued. "She was out in California, had been there for a while, I guess. I lost track of her after everything happened when I was a kid, and it wasn't like I could just look her up on Facebook or some shit like that. Apparently, she kept track of me, though. She didn't ask for money, didn't ask for anything, really. She just didn't know what to do with this other kid that she had. This eleven-year-old. Eleven years old, and I didn't even know he existed. Aiden and Brendon didn't know either, not that Brendon was actually related to the kid, but sometimes, I forget that Brendon's not my biological brother. You know?" Violet nodded in answer, and I continued.

"Aiden wanted nothing to do with my mom at the time. He told me if I left, I deserved whatever I got. He said we were making a life out here, and to go back to Mom would just fuck everything up. Because you see, I didn't know that she had a kid when I went out there. All I knew was that she needed me. And in some self-righteous, bullshit part of myself, I wanted to make sure she was okay. I didn't want her to die alone, you see. And so, Aiden said that if I walked out, that was it. That I would be choosing her over the family we had made. I didn't think about it like that, I just thought about the fact that I wanted that part of our past not to die alone. And so, I left."

Violet's eyes widened. "So, you're saying Aiden didn't know about Dillon at all? I find that hard to believe."

"As soon as I found out about Dillon, I tried to contact Aiden, even Brendon. But they wouldn't answer my calls. And I was too busy trying to figure out how to raise this eleven-year-old while feeling like a kid myself. And I didn't really keep trying to contact them after about a year." I paused. "I told Jack and Rose, though. At least over the phone. They understood, but then I was selfish and made them promise that they wouldn't tell Aiden. I was so pissed at him for not helping me when I needed it, and I didn't want to hurt him. Or maybe I wanted to hurt myself. I don't know, but Aiden never answered my calls, he pushed me away just like I pushed him away. And so, in the end, I was out in California, trying to start a new life and raise this kid."

I paused, swallowing hard. "Mom died about a year and a half after I moved out there. OD'd again, but that was the final time. I barely scraped enough money together to cremate her because it was cheaper than a burial out there. Dillon still has her ashes. I wanted nothing to do with them. I don't even know if Aiden knows about the ashes. Hell, that's probably something else I should tell him." I let out a sigh and rubbed my temple. "Everything's really fucked up. And it has been fucked up for a long time. And so, I left. I left Denver, and I left you. Because I couldn't say goodbye to you. I didn't know how."

"Cameron."

Violet's voice was soft, and I could see her shaking. I didn't know if it was sympathy or rage. Or maybe it was a mixture of both.

Her shoulders lifted and fell as she took deep, gulping breaths, and then she looked at me, and I knew that there was just rage there.

"Really? Really? You could've just said it. You could've just told me. I wasn't going to break because you needed to leave for your family. No, I broke because you didn't have the decency to say goodbye. That's why it hurts to look at you. That's why every time I see you, I remember everything we once had, and how you threw it all away. I'm not going to hold taking care of your family against you. I'll never hate you for wanting to make sure that little boy was okay. But I can hate you a little for how you did it all. I can hate you a bit for how it broke me into a million pieces and left me shattered on the floor.

"And that's why you need to go. Because I don't think you can be here right now. And I think I need to breathe."

There was nothing else to say right then. I had told Violet why I left, which, in retrospect, was a stupid decision. But I hadn't known what else to do at the time, and I had messed everything up. There was no amount of atonement that would make that okay.

So, I stood up and left, closing the door softly behind me. I just hoped that she would lock it and keep herself safe. But then again, it wasn't my responsibility to keep her safe. I had nothing to do with Violet. Our lives might have been tangled once, but it didn't mean they had to continue being so.

I didn't know what direction I was headed—not physically or emotionally. But no matter what, it wasn't going to be with Violet.

It couldn't be.

CHAPTER SEVEN

You're a mess. But then again, so am I
- Allison in a text to Violet

VIOLET

TO SAY I was not ready for today would be an understatement. But there was no getting away from this. There was no running from anything. Allison needed us, even if I wasn't sure exactly what that meant anymore.

Harmony stood on one side of me, Sienna on the other, and I wondered how it had all come to this.

Death wasn't supposed to be easy, life was hard, after all. But what was left behind seemed to be the hardest, at least in my recent experience.

Allison was gone, her life cut far too short by her own hands. And I still didn't know why she had done what she did. Maybe there wouldn't be any answers. Perhaps there didn't need to be. Maybe those answers were only for her, and even though I was the one left behind, it didn't mean that it was all about me.

Because it wasn't. Of course, it wasn't.

And today wasn't about me either. It wasn't about the fact that my chest felt too tight, or that my palms were clammy. It wasn't about the fact that I knew a migraine would come on eventually, or that I felt like I was going to throw up if I didn't focus.

It wasn't about any of that.

No, today was about saying goodbye to Allison once more and cleaning out everything that she had once loved and owned.

It still shocked me a little that Allison didn't have a will. But because of that, her parents had been in charge of everything, though they had left this part up to me and my friends and family. Allison's parents were already dealing with enough, compartmentalizing the fact that their daughter was gone and they had no answers. They had handled the funeral, the casket, dealt with watching their daughter be laid to rest, inch by inch as she was put into the ground.

They'd held the wake at their own house. They had fielded the questions, confronted being strong in the face of insurmountable pain.

And though I didn't agree with exactly how they had

handled everything, it wasn't my place to say anything. But what *was* my place, was making sure that they didn't have to deal with any more than they already had. Because while I lost my friend, they had lost their daughter.

They had lost their only child, their baby girl. And I would do anything to make sure they didn't feel any more pain from that.

So, Sienna, Harmony, and I were going to clean every inch of Allison's place and make it ready for the next tenant.

Somehow, we were going to make this place that still smelled of Allison no longer have even a single inch of her. There would be no remnants of the woman that I loved, no remnants of the best friend who had held me when I cried, who'd helped me through my migraines, and through college when I thought that I was making a mistake in my chosen field.

Allison was always the strong one, but I hadn't been able to see beneath the surface. I hadn't been able to see that something else was going on with her.

And I'd never forgive myself for that.

"Where do we begin?" Sienna asked, her voice hesitant.

"We start where we need to. So, we have boxes, and we'll put things into piles." Harmony clasped her hands in front of herself, her voice sounding far stronger than I thought it could. After all, Harmony had done this with her husband's things. Apparently, she was an expert at this now.

The fact that there was that much knowledge while dealing with loss at our ages just pissed me off.

"So, what kind of piles are you thinking?" I hadn't really done this before, not really. And I really wasn't in the mood to think about it now. But we didn't have a choice.

"Well, there're things that we'll want to keep for ourselves, there're things that her parents may like, there're things to donate, things to sell. And, obviously, there may be some things to throw away. There'll also probably be a pile that we have no idea what to do with, but we'll come back to that later. It really just depends on what there is. I know it's going to be hard, and it'll suck. But that's why we have wine for later, and that's why we don't have to do it all right now. We can do a little bit, and then a little bit later. As long as we do it in steps, we'll be okay." She took a deep breath. "We're going to be okay."

I inhaled deeply just as she had and then wrapped my arm around Harmony's shoulders. I kissed her head and closed my eyes, resting my temple against hers. Sienna wrapped her arms around both of us, and we just stood there, the three of us as a unit. A troop against what was coming next, and the fact that we weren't four. We would never be four again. And it sucked.

"I guess we should get started?" I asked, my voice low. I really didn't want to start. I just wanted to go home and wrap myself in a blanket and forget that any of this ever happened. But there was no ignoring this. There would never be any forgetting this. How could that actually be when every single time I looked in the mirror, I remembered that I had walked in to see my best friend in the entire world no longer with us.

Because there was no turning back from that.

"Like I said, piles. Maybe we should start with the living room? I don't know if we're ready for the bedroom yet. That might be too personal."

"Everything's going to be personal here," Sienna said wisely. "Even the bathroom's going to have stuff that she used every day. Like her lotions and everything that reminds me of her. I just hate this. I want to know...I want to know why. I want to know why she's gone. And I know we'll probably never find out, and I hate it. It just makes me so angry." Sienna threw her hands into the air. I reached out to my little sister but stopped when she glared at me.

"Sienna." I didn't know what else to say. There were no words for this.

"No, just don't. Just let me be angry and a little whiny right now. I think I need that. I'll let you do the same when you reach this part of the grief. Because I still think that you're in that numb part right now, Violet. The part that hurts. I was there for a while. But I keep moving around from each set to another."

"Stages of grief are crap," Harmony said, her voice low.

"What?" I asked, confused.

"There aren't just stages you randomly move through. No, you feel it all. You feel every single little part at all times, at every single point of the day. Sometimes, you move forward, sometimes, you move two steps back. It's not a gradual progression, so everything is perfectly fine eventually. Because it's not going to be fine. You're never going to be fine. But, eventually, you might be okay with who you are as you find your way to breathe again. But there are no stages of grief. There's just grief. Plain and simple. And there's nothing simple about it. There is grief. There is loss. And there is you, finding a way to live through it and knowing that everything hurts around you. So, everything's going to hurt. You're going to be angry. You're going to be sad. You're going to be numb. You're going to be all of it. And that's okay. It's okay to feel all of that. Or nothing. It's just okay."

I stared at my friend, wondering why she hadn't said any of this before. But, then again, when would she have been able to? We hadn't understood what she felt when she lost her husband. I still didn't. I would never be able to feel that, and I swore I never wanted to. We had lost Allison, and it was a different kind of grief, but it was still grief. We were just trying to find our way.

Someone cleared their throat from the doorway, and we all turned to see the Connolly brothers standing there, looking awkward as if they had heard Harmony's entire speech.

From the way Brendon was looking at her, I figured that they had heard every single word.

And I had no idea what we were going to do about it.

Not that I really knew about anything anymore. But that was enough of those self-pitying thoughts. There were important things to get done today, and feeling bad about myself wasn't one of them.

And, speaking of feeling bad, I noticed exactly who was here. Brendon, Aiden, *and* Cameron were standing there. The only one missing was Dillon, but then again, he wasn't a Connolly, was he? I didn't even know Dillon's last name.

I hadn't asked many questions, or how old exactly Dillon was—though I figured he was eighteen if I did the math right about Cameron's story. I hadn't asked what Dillon's plans were, or what Cameron's plans were when it came to the kid. I hadn't asked any of it because I'd been too hurt about having to remember exactly how I had felt when Cameron left all those years ago. Yes, maybe that made me selfish for those few moments, but I needed that. Because he had been selfish, and I hadn't really wanted to lash out at him, but I needed those few moments to regain a bit of the person I had become when I put myself back together after losing him. I might not like every part of myself, but I had enough respect for myself to be okay.

"You guys showed up," Sienna said quickly, moving forward. "I know you said you were, but I was afraid that you would get busy or decide that it was just going to be too hard. But, thanks for coming." Sienna reached out and hugged Brendon and then Cameron and then Aiden. And because Sienna had done it, Harmony moved forward and did the same, saying something soft to each of the brothers that I couldn't really hear.

"We're here for you if you need us. We like you guys. Just wanted to make sure you knew that."

"Thank you for coming," I said softly. I guess we're going to need help with the heavy lifting, after all.

"Do you have a moving truck or anything?" Aiden asked, frowning as he looked around the space. He had once loved Allison, and I didn't know how he felt standing in the place where she had once lived that had nothing to do with him. Everything was just so complicated and connected, it was hard for me to truly understand what anyone was feeling when I didn't even know what *I* was feeling.

"No moving truck today," I said, trying to keep my voice strong. It wasn't easy when all I wanted to do was break down. But I had done that enough recently. Today, I would work, and then I would get drunk. Really fucking drunk.

"So, it's just packing up? When are you planning on the moving truck?" Cameron asked, looking at me and then pointedly looking away. I knew it wasn't anger that I saw in his eyes. He was just trying to give me space. But I really didn't have time to deal with any extra feelings right now.

"We have some time, and I don't want to do too much at once," Harmony said. "Today's all about piles, maybe packing some things up. We brought some boxes."

Brendon cleared his throat. "I did too, just in case. But you don't have to use them if you don't want to." He added that last part almost as an afterthought, and I wondered why

Brendon was acting so weird. Then again, I didn't really know him anymore. Maybe he was always this way.

"I'm sure we'll need them. We always need a lot more boxes than we think at first. Anyway, we were thinking about starting in the living room." Harmony looked sad and confused as she looked around. "And I don't really think we can split up on this, because I think it's something that we need to work on together to make decisions. I know what everyone thinks, and I know what I'm doing here because I have some experience, but I really am out of my depth. If anyone else has any ideas, I would really appreciate hearing them."

I moved forward and hugged my friend close. "I'm here for you. Always. And, don't worry, we'll figure it out. How about everybody take one corner of the living room, maybe work in pairs, and we'll just go through everything piece by piece. Some things are going to be easier than others, some things might take some discussion. And we don't have to do it all today. We just have to get started. We just have to get started." I repeated the last part, knowing it was for me. It sucked, it all just sucked. There really wasn't another word for it.

Somehow, I ended up working with Cameron, and I didn't know if my friends and sister had meant to do that or if it was just by happenstance. Brendon knew Harmony the best, so he worked with her and was so gentle with how he helped her. I figured that he knew that every single moment she was thinking about losing Allison, she was probably thinking about her late-husband, too. I knew I was.

Aiden and Sienna worked together, the pair quiet yet the only two laughing softly as they looked at things. They had known Allison the best, even though Allison was also my best friend. It was sometimes hard to remember that. Hard to remember that Allison had touched more than just one person. She had affected the lives of so many, and yet here we were, without her.

A hand grazed my shoulder, and I didn't move away. I couldn't. "These are her picture albums," Cameron said softly. "Why don't we stack these, and you guys can look at them later?"

I shook my head quickly. "Box them, and then we can take them to my house or something. I'll look at them later. *Way* later. I don't think any of us are ready for that right now."

The others had been listening and agreed quickly, and Cameron boxed them up so I didn't have to touch them, so I wouldn't have to look at them. Maybe it made me weak, perhaps it made me shallow, but it hurt to think about everything, and I just needed some space. Just needed time to breathe.

We worked for three hours, slowly putting things into piles.

It was weird to think about putting someone's life into a pile. I didn't even know if I could do that for myself.

What was the pile of old bills that were already paid?

What about the stack of DVDs that she had watched at one time, but no one really needed anymore?

There were the CDs that hadn't been thrown away when she went fully to digital. There were random knick-knacks that people had given to her over time, or those I knew she had gotten from friends, or when she traveled. There were picture frames all over, Allison's smiling face looking down at us as if she had held a secret that I didn't know.

But I guess that was the case, after all.

There was so much we had missed, and I didn't want to miss anything anymore. I didn't want to miss any of it.

There was the TV, of course, and all her electronics. I had no idea what to do with some of the stuff. But Aiden, Brendon, and Cameron figured out where she kept her old boxes in the back and packaged those up. We would likely either sell or donate them since none of us really needed or wanted them.

"Would Dillon need any of this?" I asked, my voice soft. "I mean after we talk to Allison's parents. I don't know what Dillon's plans are, but maybe he would like something to start out?" I didn't realize I'd said the words out loud, or that I'd even thought them until they were already out for everyone to hear. Harmony and Sienna both gave me soft smiles as if they were happy with what I had asked. But I really wasn't sure I'd done the right thing. Aiden glared and then turned away, not answering. Brendon gave me a similar smile to the girls' as if he'd been thinking along the same lines but hadn't spoken up. But it was Cameron who spoke first.

"Eventually, he's going off to college," he said quickly. "This is just a gap year for reasons I can get into later." He sounded a bit angry about that, but I didn't press. Not yet. "But, maybe? Let's see what Allison's parents say first, and then we can talk about it. I think that's really generous. Really generous."

"Allison's parents said that we could have anything we wanted in here, that they wanted nothing to do with it. But I'll double-check. I kind of like the idea of something that she enjoyed being used with something that a friend might like. I don't know, maybe I'm just getting sentimental." I sighed, stacking up the greeting cards from the latest holiday that Allison hadn't tossed yet.

"You're allowed to be sentimental. You're allowed to feel whatever you need to," Cameron whispered, and I ignored him. Or, at least I tried to. I was a little too confused to make any decisions right then. But at least I was trying to think of the future, trying to think of someone other than myself.

"I don't understand why there wasn't a note," Sienna said quickly, anger back in her voice. "Why didn't she tell us? Why didn't we see it?" Aiden wrapped his arm around her shoulders, and Brendon looked at them both as I tried to find the words. I just didn't have any. How could I?

Because I'd been thinking the same questions this whole time.

"Sometimes, there are notes. Sometimes, we don't get the answers in life. Sometimes, we just don't know."

I wiped the tears from my face and didn't pull back when Cameron leaned into me, giving me as much comfort as I would allow.

"And that's a really crappy thing to say. And I really need a drink. Does anyone need a drink? I could really use a drink."

Everyone was silent for a moment before they all got up and looked ready to go.

"How about we drive back to our places, and I'll set up some ride shares to get us back to the bar? That way, we can drink to our hearts' content and not worry about driving." Brendon was already looking down at his phone at something, and I just nodded, knowing that was probably the best answer to everything.

"Usually, I just drink alone at home," I said quickly and then laughed. "But that makes me sound sad."

Brendon snorted. "No, that makes you sound like any other American who lives alone. We just happen to own a bar so we can make drinking in public feel like you're drinking alone. But we'll have a drink in Allison's honor, and we'll try to make it to the next day. How does that sound?"

I looked at Cameron, wondering why we were always in each other's presence when I knew that we should stay away. But it wasn't as easy as just walking away like he had before. And yet, it hadn't exactly been easy then either.

"Let's go, then. Let's go see what we can do so we can make it to the next day."

And maybe that would be our new slogan for the rest of this period. What could we do to make it to the next day? Because Allison hadn't made it to her next day.

And, somehow, I would have to make it for the both of us.

CHAPTER EIGHT

CAMERON

IT WAS PROBABLY around the second drink of the night that I realized that we shouldn't be here. That drinking away our worries wasn't going to help anything in the long-run. But considering that I was already a little numb where it counted, I knew the others had to be way further down the rabbit hole.

Because, yes, I had known Allison, and I missed her. Going through her things was hard, and I'd hated every bit of it, but watching Violet and the others deal with it, each of their emotions playing out on their faces so bright and vivid that it hurt to even think about...that was harder.

There wasn't anything I could do about it though, except to keep drinking and make sure that the others didn't drink too much. We had each taken a car service so we could get home safely, but I knew none of us wanted to deal with the aftereffects of a hangover. We weren't in our early twenties anymore, and drinking too much and feeling bad the next day wasn't really something that any of us needed to put ourselves through.

But nobody really seemed to mind just then.

Thankfully, we were in the back room next to the pool tables so others wouldn't be able to witness our drunken debauchery unless they came back here. And they never seemed to since we weren't busy.

Brendon brought by some shots, probably making our third drink of the night, even though I think we might've been on our fourth at this point. I wasn't really sure. Maybe our fifth.

It was tequila, my arch-nemesis because I was usually an Irish whiskey kind of guy. But since we started with tequila, that meant I couldn't add any more liquor. Just beer and tequila. I'd probably throw up later, but it'd be better than adding whiskey on top of it. Or even something stronger or sweeter.

My stomach rolled. Yeah, best not to remember that night when I was barely twenty-one and drank way too many fruity drinks alongside Violet. She hadn't wanted to drink alone, so I had been stupid and said that I would drink the same thing she was.

We both ended up lying on the bathroom floor, sick, pale, and not wanting to touch each other, even though we had both promised to have the hottest sex of our lives.

That'd taken another three days to get to, considering that we had both been hungover for more than forty hours.

Jesus, I'd been young. Too young.

"Okay, this shot is for us. For the fact that we're here. Together." Brendon held up his shot, and I did the same, doing my best not to remember that sweet-tasting drunk night as I looked at my brother and then the rest of them. Aiden had his arm around the back of Sienna's chair as the two of them laughed, telling some joke that none of us heard, but was apparently hilarious to the two of them. Sienna held up her other arm, grinning. And, for the first time, I thought the expression might just reach her eyes. Though not fully. I didn't know when that would happen, but I hoped it did soon.

Harmony sat between Brendon and Violet, rolling her eyes as she held up her shot. For some reason, I didn't think she was going to be as drunk as the rest of us. Either she wasn't finishing her drinks, or she had a higher tolerance for liquor than any of us did. Considering that the Connolly brothers could drink almost anybody under the table, that was saying something.

Violet sat by me and gave me a look that went straight to my balls. Yes, I was an idiot for even thinking that, and I knew she was drunk—I was on my way to being drunk, too. But she was so damn sexy. Always had been. And I could never resist her. So, I was going to do my best tonight to just keep drinking and do that whole resisting thing that I wasn't very good at.

"Yes, I'll drink to that." And then we all took the shots and banged our glasses on the table, though not too hard, thankfully. After all, this was our bar, and I didn't want to break shit.

Considering that it was a Saturday night, it should have been busier than it was, but it wasn't, and that worried me. I knew that all of us were working on ideas for how to increase the bar's presence and keep it afloat, but right then, with a couple of empty chairs at the bar, and the fact that it should've been filled to the rafters with people, it worried me. So, I sipped at my beer and tried not to worry. That could be left for tomorrow. God knew I stewed enough for everybody here.

As did Brendon. And Aiden.

Aiden took a bite of the nachos that Beckham had brought to the table earlier and frowned.

"They aren't using my recipe," Aiden grumbled. "What's the point of me telling them what to do when they won't fucking do it?"

"Maybe you shouldn't curse at them and growl?" Sienna asked, batting her eyelashes like she was so sweet.

"I am fucking nice. And a damn good boss," Aiden said before he took another bite of the nachos and scowled.

"I think they taste just fine, Aiden," Harmony said, dipping her chip into some sour cream. "I mean, yours are better, we all know that because you are a god of cooking, but these aren't bad."

"Yes, because whenever you want to think about good

food that brings people in, you want the phrase 'not bad' as part of that." Aiden let out a sigh and stood up, a little wobbly. Okay, apparently, we might've been on drink six. I wasn't really sure anymore. "I should go back there and tell them what they're doing wrong."

I reached out over Sienna and tugged on my twin's arm. "No, you can do that tomorrow. When we're sober, probably hungover, and not acting like assholes. Don't go back there when you're drunk and start yelling at people. Number one, it's probably not the best thing for our staff to see us like this when they're working and we're not, and number two, it's probably going to break like thirty health laws. So, don't fuck up and just sit down."

Aiden glowered at me before doing as I suggested. "Well, that's all nice and dandy for you, but at least you have someone running the bar when you're not there, someone who actually knows what the fuck he's doing."

I turned as Aiden lifted his beer in cheers toward Beckham. The bearded bartender just rolled his eyes and toasted with his bottle of water. Thankfully, Beckham didn't drink when he was on duty. The bartender who worked with Beckham before I came back had done a few too many taste-tests throughout the evening. So much, in fact, that he was basically a drunk loser who spent all his time trying to get wasted with the college co-eds instead of actually working.

I had fired him quickly, and Beckham had done his best to pick up the slack when I was trying to figure out my way in the new place. I knew Jack hadn't wanted things to go downhill, but he had been sick, and there was only so much he could do on his own after Rose died.

And my brothers and I hadn't been here to help.

So, it was my fault that everything was like it was now. And we were going to fix it. I just hated the fact that we were changing everything to make it happen. Because there had to be some things that Jack loved that had worked out. No, the food wasn't as good as it used to be, and that was because of the old cooks that we used to have. And maybe one of the current ones we still had if the nachos were anything to go by tonight.

And, no, we didn't have some of the new craft beers that I wanted. But I was getting some of them in and using some of my connections back in California to get it done. A lot of the local bars had the Denver local brews because it was Colorado and we were sort of at the center of the whole thing. But I wanted something different. So, I would try to get some of the Colorado brews, and some of the California ones. It was harder than it sounded, but I was making it happen.

Brendon, however, was doing his best to try and get people here in snazzy ways. Ways I really wasn't in the mood for. But it wasn't my place to say anything. It was never my place to say.

"You know, that wing night I'm working on, that's going to be good for us. We just need to get the word out." Brendon chugged the rest of his beer and then stood up. "Speaking of wing night, let's go play pool."

I snorted, finishing the last of my beer. "How the hell do those two things go together?"

"They do because I say they do." Brendon raised his chin and held out his arm as if he were a duke in the Regency era. "My lady, does thou want to play pool?"

Dear God, my brother was an idiot. A very big idiot.

"You're drunk," Harmony said, laughing as she stood up. But she put her hand on his arm anyway and did a little curtsy as if she were wearing one of those long dresses, even though she was in jeans. "I would love to beat your ass at pool."

"Those are fighting words, my lady."

"My lady?" Aiden asked. "Seriously?" He looked down at Sienna and glowered. "You want to go beat their asses, short stack?"

Sienna blinked. "Seriously? Harmony gets *my lady*, and I get short stack? Why don't you just call me the lovely troll or the court jester at this point?" Sienna tossed her hair back from her shoulders and stood up, pushing past Aiden to get to the pool area.

I looked over at Violet, who was laughing behind her beer at the four of them. "So, you want to play?"

"What? I'm not a fair lady or even a court jester? I'm just a whatever?" She finished her beer and set the glass down.

"Well, you're Violet. Figured us going over there and kicking their asses as a duo was probably better than watching them fall all over each other because they're too drunk to actually see where the ball is."

"I don't think Harmony is drunk. In fact, I think that's her first beer from earlier, and she's just doing tequila shots."

I looked over at the table, noticing that, yes indeed, that was Harmony's first beer from earlier. It was probably all warm and disgusting now, but I didn't think that Harmony minded since she wasn't really drinking it.

"Well, she can beat us all, but I can't just let my brothers go in there and be idiots alone."

She snorted. "So, you have to be an idiot with them?"

I scooted my chair back and stood up, holding out my hand. "Pretty much. Let's go, Violet."

"I guess." She slid her hand into mine, and it was as if she'd always been there, as if there hadn't been a time where she wasn't in my life. But I knew that wasn't the case. I knew I had hurt her. I'd even hurt her recently. I was the asshole here, and I always would be.

"We have to make sure that at least Brendon doesn't win. Because he always gets the most arrogant when he does." I whispered the words, knowing the others would be able to hear.

"Oh, I remember. You and Aiden are pretty arrogant yourselves, though." Violet looked down at our clasped hands, and I realized that I hadn't let go of her yet. "I thought I said that we wouldn't be near each other. That you needed to go." She murmured the words, but I still heard them.

"I'm not good at doing what I'm supposed to."

"I guess I'm pretty much the same."

I let go of her hand as we entered the pool room and went for our cues. Somehow, we were just drunk enough to make a game with six people. Considering that there were only stripes and solids, it didn't make any sense, and Harmony had declared herself the winner even though Sienna was the one who had taken to standing on a chair, raising her arms, and fisting her hands in the air.

And that's when I knew that we were beyond drunk and probably needed to go home.

Thankfully, Beckham saw us and laughed as he held up his hands for our phones.

"Okay, folks, I'm going to call you guys some ride shares, and then you are going home. Don't forget to drink a glass of water while you're waiting, and then another before you go to bed. And some aspirin then and when you wake up. Because I do not want to hear you all grumbling tomorrow that you're all hungover and bitchy." He looked over at the girls. "I'm actually talking about the men, not you."

"I assumed when you said bitchy, you were talking about Aiden," Sienna said very seriously.

Aiden, for some reason, found that hysterically funny and couldn't stop laughing. I looked over at my twin, wondering when I'd actually heard him laugh last. It had to have been years ago. But, maybe, if I'd actually lived in the same state as he did, I would've heard it before this. Damn, I missed it. I'd missed so much. I'd stayed away because

Dillon needed me, but I hadn't wanted to leave. And, frankly, I'd been scared to come home. I'd fucked up more than once, and I didn't want to do it again.

So, just hanging out with my friends and my brothers, maybe that was the first step—or at least a step in the right direction.

I helped clean up the pool area and went back to the front of the bar, making sure everything was cleaned up. We were the last ones in the place, and Beckham just shook his head as he shooed everyone out.

"I got it, boss. You never get drunk or actually have fun these days. You're allowed to do it now. Nobody else really saw you like that, only me."

I nodded, holding out my hand for the other man. "Thanks, Beck. No one really needs to see us like this."

Beckham shook my hand and gave me a tight nod. "Well, sometimes, you just need a day where you can breathe. I know today must've been hard for the girls, and you guys. I didn't know Allison, but I can see from the way you guys are grieving for her that she must've been a good person."

I swallowed hard, my throat tight. "She was one of the best." I hadn't been here to know who she had become these past years, but it still didn't make any sense that the smiling girl that I had known wasn't here anymore.

But that was the thing with death, nothing made sense.

Beckham got cars for everybody, and somehow, Violet ended up in mine. I didn't really know how that had happened, but Beckham had a way about him. Either he was an idiot, or he was trying to get on my good side. Not that I actually knew if this would be good. For all I knew, this would mess everything up even more.

"Why am I at your house?" Violet asked as we got out of the ride share's car. I did my best to focus on giving the man a tip before helping Violet into the house. "I think Beckham's weird."

"Or you and Beckham have serious plans that did not involve telling me about them." She raised her chin and sauntered into my living room.

I did my best to keep my gaze off her ass, but it was very hard when she was wearing tight leggings that just seemed to mold to her butt. I really, really liked her curves, had liked them before, and I liked them even more now.

I looked around my living room, hoping I had cleaned it up at least a little bit, and then looked down at Dillon's shoes in the entryway. Shit. I had forgotten. I forgot that I wasn't alone in this house.

"Uh, we need to be quiet, Dillon's here."

She rolled her eyes and glared. "What do we have to be quiet about? Am I here for nefarious purposes?"

I snorted. And then I went up to Violet and framed her face with my hands. "We're too drunk. Way too drunk."

"Of course, we are. I think being drunk's the only way I can actually think."

And because I knew it was a mistake, I let it happen

anyway. I lowered my head and brushed my lips across hers, just a caress, for just a moment.

I had missed this. Missed this more than anything.

And when she didn't move away, I kissed her again.

This is what I'd been missing. Violet.

It'd always been her.

And I knew there was no way that she would let me continue doing this. Knew that there was no way that this was the right decision.

So I kissed her.

Because I had to.

CHAPTER NINE

Don't make any mistakes. Unless they're with me.
Then that's fine.

    - Allison in a text to Violet

VIOLET

MY HEAD WAS FUZZY, and it wasn't just because of the liquor in my system. No, it was because of the man in front of me, the one who currently had his lips pressed to mine. This was such a mistake. This was beyond a mistake. I should have found a way to get into my own ride share and gone home on my own.

But when Beckham asked me on the way back to the pool room if I wanted to get into Cameron's car or go home alone, I had said that, of course, I wanted to go with Cameron.

Yes, I was drunk, and I was making poor decisions. But, apparently, Beckham thought he was a matchmaker. And he hadn't wanted me to be forced into a situation I wasn't comfortable with.

So, yes, while he was a nice man, I was still going to beat him up. Just like I was going to hurt Cameron.

But all thoughts of that fled my mind when Cameron's hand slid through my hair to cup the back of my head and pull me closer to him. I wrapped my arms around his waist, pressing my body against his as I kissed him even harder. I had forgotten what his kisses felt like. I had forgotten what he felt like. Yes, he was larger than he had been even seven years ago, more muscular, a little sharper-edged. But he still felt like Cameron.

My Cameron.

Yes, I was drunk, but I wasn't drunk enough to actually think that he was mine.

Yet I couldn't stop kissing him.

I just wanted to feel. I just wanted to be. I didn't want to think about Allison, I didn't want to think about work, I didn't want to think about my ex-husband and his new wife, I didn't want to think about the fact that I still had to worry about the rest of Allison's stuff.

I didn't want to think about what life would be like without her.

So, I just kissed Cameron. I knew it was selfish, knew this was all a mistake.

But I didn't stop.

He was the one that pulled away first. And then he leaned his forehead against mine and let out a ragged breath.

"What are we doing?" he asked, his voice rough.

"I don't know, but I want to keep doing it."

He pulled back, his brows lowered as he frowned.

"If we do this, it's going to change everything. We're not kids anymore."

"It meant something when we were kids too, though. And I just want to feel. I know it's all complicated, and I know that this is wrong and stupid. But I have just enough liquor in me to make me brave enough to say it, though not enough where I'll be taking advantage of you, or you'll be taking advantage of me."

He studied my face. "I would say that that's just the right amount of liquor, the right amount of drunk. But I can't take advantage of you."

I moved closer, impossibly close, so we were pressed against one another and I could feel the hard ridge of him on my thigh. "Personal advantage here. It's just you and me. And you're helping me feel. I miss feeling. Can you do that? We can deal with the tomorrows tomorrow. We can deal with everything that's going to hurt. But I just miss people. I miss being held. I just miss it all."

I miss you.

I didn't say that. I couldn't. Because I was afraid if I did,

Cameron would see too much. Because I still loved him, and I hated that. Maybe it was a different kind of love, maybe it wasn't the part that meant I was *in* love with him. I had moved on from that and pieced myself back together after he left. And though he'd apologized and groveled, I didn't know if that was enough yet.

But it was just enough that I could want to lean into him, and I needed to be held. And maybe I was taking advantage of him, but from the way his eyes darkened and the way he let out a slow growl, I knew that he wanted me as much as I wanted him. Hell, I could feel how hard he was, yes, he wanted me just as much as I wanted him.

I didn't say anything else just then, and I knew it was because, if we spoke, we would just break the bubble that meant everything would be okay, and that this was just for right now. Because it wasn't going to be. There would be ramifications, but we would deal with them tomorrow.

My head was swimming, the mixture of the booze and Cameron filling me up, so I just closed my eyes and leaned into him as he took my lips again. He tasted of beer, a little tequila, and even some nachos. He just tasted of Cameron. I loved it. Or at least I *had* loved it. Maybe I just missed it.

Maybe I just missed touching.

I had been married since I was last with Cameron, I'd been in other relationships. Cameron wasn't my only, far from it, but he had been my first love, my first everything.

So, having him hold me right then felt like coming home a bit.

There was a reason that taking advantage was something that happened.

Sometimes, you just needed.

So, I kissed him back, wanting more, *needing* more.

"If we're going to do this, we can't do it out here. Dillon could walk in at any moment."

This. He was talking about sex. Something that I was also talking about. Okay, I could do this. I'd had sex before. I'd had lots of sex. I'd had lots of sex with *Cameron* before. This wouldn't be anything new. It wasn't going to be scary. It would be exactly what I needed.

And I was going to thank God that I had just enough booze in my system just then so I could make this happen. Because it's what I needed. What I wanted.

"I forgot about Dillon."

Cameron let out a rough chuckle. "You make me forget about a lot of things." And then he leaned down, put his arm under my legs, and lifted me up to his chest. I let out a little screech and put my hand over my mouth so I wouldn't get any louder. I didn't want to wake up Dillon, an eighteen-year-old boy who would know exactly what his brother and I were doing. I did not need to deal with that embarrassment anytime soon.

Cameron grinned, and he looked just like his younger self. No worries. And that's what we both needed. Just us.

I knew that the word *us* held baggage far beyond just two letters put together to make a word. But I was going to ignore all of that. And because I had enough alcohol in my system, I could.

And so, I let my hand go and brushed the back of my fingers along his bearded cheek. His jaw was defined, square and a little angular. It had been that way before, but now it looked even more masculine.

And while he and Aiden might be twins, I had always loved the way Cameron looked more. Maybe because he smiled more. Perhaps because I loved the way Cameron looked at *me*. He had always looked at me as if I were the best thing that had ever happened to him. I had never really believed that. Never really thought that I could ever be that for anybody. But it had been true, even in the short time that we were together.

Cameron wasn't looking at me exactly like that now, but I understood that he would never do that. Because we weren't who we were before. We were who we were now, and I was just going to live in the moment, just be with him with his arms around me. He carried me down the hallway, both of us quiet and looking at each other. Neither of us wanted to wake up his brother and ruin the moment. Neither of us wanted to say anything or think too hard and ruin the moment that way either.

When we got into the bedroom, he set me down and kissed me again, this time a little rougher, a little harder. I could feel the need in that kiss, the desire in his touch.

His hands trailed over my body, and I arched into him,

pulling my mouth back and moving my head to the side. His lips latched on to my skin, licking and biting and sucking along my neck and down to my shoulder. He tugged at my jacket, and I did the same to his, both of the garments pooling to the floor. I was only wearing flats and could easily slip out of my shoes, and that made it easier for me to go up onto my tiptoes and bring his mouth down for another searing kiss.

His hands moved to my butt, and he molded me with his large grip. Then he pulled me closer, pelvis to pelvis so I could feel the hard ridge of him against the heat of myself. I wanted him inside of me, wanted him on top of me, below me, anywhere near me. I needed this, craved it.

It had been so long since I had been with anyone, far longer since I had been with Cameron. And I didn't want to wait any longer. I slid my fingers under his shirt, reveling in the hard ridges of his abdomen. He was sculpted, easily had an eight pack, and it made me want to giggle. He was like one of those cover models in the books I loved, but he was all real. There was nothing fantastical about him. He was real, and all mine for the night.

I scraped my fingernails down his skin, and he let out a slight groan, shivering under my touch. And when I put my hand on the hem of his shirt and tugged. He let me slide it over his head, lifting his arms for me.

"Wow," I whispered, my voice a little shaky with awe.

"You like?" he asked, flexing for me. I laughed, unable to hold myself back.

I loved laughing when I had sex. I just loved being. I

loved the fact that Cameron could make me smile and do stupid things to make me feel like there were no worries in the world even when we were on the verge of something more.

The booze in my system seemed to rev me up, and I leaned forward, licking his nipple. He let out a shuddering sigh, and I bit down before going to his other pec. He was tattooed, a few down his side and one over his shoulder. He didn't have too many, and I knew his brothers had more, at least they had back when we were younger. When I moved behind him to look at his back, I noticed that he had a couple more that he didn't have back then.

There were no women's names, no female faces. And for that, I was grateful. But there were a few jagged-looking tears along his side, and I wondered who they were for. For him? For his family? For his mom?

I didn't ask. Instead, I kissed his spine all the way down to the top of his jeans. And then I stood back up and leaned around to kiss his lips. He kept kissing me, and I fell into him, loving the way we were going slow, feeling one another. He had his hands under my shirt, undoing my bra even as I still wore my blouse, and I just grinned. He had always been very good at that.

Soon, I was naked from the top up, my breasts in his hands as he sucked one nipple into his mouth, using his fingers to play with the other.

Each suck and little bite went straight to my core, and I knew my panties were wet for him. I knew I needed him.

"I need you," I whispered, not meaning to actually say the words. Cameron could know that I needed him, could know that I wanted him. But just in body, not in soul.

I needed to remember that.

Cameron leaned back and winked before going to his knees. My eyes widened when he kissed his way down my chest, my belly, to right above the waistband of my pants.

With one hand, he slowly slid his finger along the elastic, not quite lowering them. He used the other to untie one of his shoes, then the other. And then he was barefoot, his pants undone, and slowly sliding mine down my body. He cupped my butt as he did it, and then kissed my core over my panties before stripping me completely out of my pants.

And then I stood there in my underwear, looking down at him and sliding my hand through his hair.

Cameron had always been good with oral sex, and while I liked giving him head, I knew he enjoyed eating me out even more.

To say I had been a lucky girl would be an understatement.

And, no, I was not going to remember everything that came after when he left—the pain, the breaking. Because that wasn't going to happen again. This was just one time. This was just Cameron and me. No promises, no memories.

Cameron kissed me over the top of my panties again and then slowly pushed them back so he could kiss me where I wanted him most.

I let out a groan, throwing my head back and almost

falling right down on my butt because there was nothing to hold me up except for his very strong arm. Thank God for Cameron and those strong arms.

"I'm going to fall if you keep doing that," I panted.

"I'll catch you."

And he would, but then I remembered the time he hadn't. But I pushed that out of my mind. Instead of relying on him, though, I took a few steps back and leaned against the edge of the bed, spreading my legs so he could see me.

He grinned and then crawled towards me. Crawling was a good step. Almost like groveling. I'd take it.

And then he kissed me again, this time lower. I groaned, my head rolling back, my eyes closing. He sucked and licked and then he used his fingers. And when I came, my legs were wrapped around his head, and I was groaning, hearing his name on my lips as I tried to keep quiet so Dillon wouldn't overhear.

Soon, Cameron was above me, stripping off his pants as he gripped the base of his cock in his hand.

"You look so fucking beautiful." He groaned. He was growling his words, a glare on his face, his eyes narrowed. For some reason, that was really sexy. He probably shouldn't have looked sexy, should have looked very scary, but I couldn't help my reaction. This was Cameron. And I was always far too weak when it came to him.

"Well, what are you going to do now?" I asked, my voice low and kind of sultry. I hadn't meant to sound like that, but it was Cameron. Again, I couldn't help myself. Before he could answer, though, I sat up. I was on my knees, shaking, and I pulled at his thighs so he could come closer. His eyes widened, and then he smirked. Oh, I loved that smirk. Because he didn't always mean it, but I knew it meant naughty things.

And speaking of naughty, I opened my mouth and swallowed him whole. He groaned, his hands sliding through my hair as he slowly worked his way in and out of my mouth. I used one palm to cup his balls, the other to wrap around the base of him because I couldn't actually swallow all of him.

I flattened my tongue and hummed, knowing exactly what he liked, or at least how he used to enjoy it. And from the way he groaned, the way he shook, I knew he still did. And then he pulled out and kissed me again, his whole body quaking.

"If you keep doing that, I'm not going to last. I'm not as young as I once was."

"Neither am I, but I don't mind."

And then I leaned back and spread myself for him.

He groaned and then went to the nightstand, slipping a condom down his shaft. Thank God he had remembered because I had forgotten.

I had always used condoms with my exes, except for my ex-husband and Cameron. My ex-husband and I never used condoms once we got married because I had thought we were trying to have a baby. Cameron and I had stopped using condoms after we were both tested and I had gone on birth control.

We were not those people anymore. We were not in a committed relationship, and I didn't know if he had been tested or not. I had, but I still wanted to be careful. It didn't matter that I was on birth control, I needed that barrier. I needed far more than just that barrier if I were honest.

And then he was over me, sliding into me as he met my gaze.

I groaned, my entire body shivering as he filled me up. His mouth was on me just for a moment before he pulled back to look at me.

And when I looked into his eyes, I felt barer than I could ever remember, even when I was naked. It didn't matter that I was still wearing my panties and he had just moved them off to the side, it didn't matter that we had been intimate like this before.

Because this was different, this was new. This was nothing like it had been before.

Yet it felt like it should have been.

And that scared me. That scared me more than anything I could have possibly felt just then. And then he moved. He moved slowly and so sweetly that I could almost forget that I was supposed to be scared, forget that I wasn't supposed to be here. He moved, and I moved with him, and when we both came, I called his name, his mouth on mine, taking my shout.

Everything felt like it had before, only different. Like time had passed and we weren't exactly the same people that we had once been. Because we weren't.

We fell into each other twice that night, exhausted and no longer drunk. But it was like we both knew if we stopped, if we pulled away, that would be it. That it would be the end again. I was afraid to know what would happen when we did.

I fell asleep on his chest, holding him close as he held me so tightly, I knew I would likely be a little bruised in the morning. But I didn't care because I needed this night, even if it scared me.

When I woke up the next morning, my head pounded, and I knew a migraine might be coming on a little bit later and not just from the drinks. I knew I had made a mistake.

There was no more booze in my system, no more shots of tequila to help me make this better.

I was in bed, completely naked, and completely sated by Cameron Connolly.

I had promised myself that I wouldn't let this happen, but I had because I'd needed someone, and he had been there. Because he had always been there, except for the one time when it had truly mattered.

I hated this, and I hated how I felt. Because I blamed myself for this. I was the one who'd said that everything would be okay, even though I knew it would hurt.

What the hell was I going to do?

Cameron was still sleeping, out of it, and I knew if I moved, he wouldn't actually wake up.

Thankfully, he was still a hard-sleeper, so I rolled out of bed and pulled on my panties, remembering how he had pulled them off the second time we made love. No, not making love. It was just sex. There was nothing about love. We were not in love. We were not in a relationship. Everything would be fine.

I pulled on the rest of my clothes and tried to put my hair back into a bun even though I knew I looked like it was the morning after. It was, after all.

I didn't know if I was supposed to leave a note or pretend that everything was okay, but Cameron knew where I was, knew where I lived. And I knew that this wasn't the end. I knew that we would have to talk about it. But not this morning. Not when my head hurt, and I was afraid that I was going to throw up. Not because of the hangover, but because of an oncoming migraine.

I quickly tiptoed out of his room and called a ride service so I'd be able to get back to my house. I picked up my purse from the front entryway table, having forgotten that I'd left it there, and then I looked up at the sound of someone clearing their throat.

Oh, of course. *Of course.*

"Oh, hi, Dillon."

Dillon took a bite of his cereal and lifted a brow. Then he swallowed and smiled. "Hey there, Violet. Need a ride?"

He was very subtly trying to let me get out of this quickly, but I still had no idea what to say to him. "No, my driver should be here soon. Um, bye." I scurried out of the house and waited on the side of the road for my driver to pick me up.

Last night had been one of the best and worst times of my life. And I knew it was only the beginning. Because there was no going back to the way things were.

Though I didn't know where they were going from now on either.

CHAPTER TEN

CAMERON

WAKING up in the morning all alone because the woman you'd been sleeping next to most of the night had tiptoed her way out without waking you wasn't the best way to start your day. And it had all gone downhill from there.

I pinched the bridge of my nose, trying to calmly let out a breath, but I couldn't help it. I was just so fucking tired.

I'd rolled over that morning and put out my hand so I could touch Violet, so I could make sure that everything that had happened the night before was real, but Violet wasn't there. She had left.

Maybe I should have expected it, and somewhere deep down I had, but it was still a bit of a shock to open my eyes and realize that she wasn't there.

I'd stumbled out of bed myself, rubbing my eyes with the heel of my hand as I shoved myself back into my jeans, at least doing up the zipper if not the button. I had thought that maybe she was still in the house, maybe getting coffee or just sitting on the couch, wondering what the hell we had done.

As soon as I'd gone out there, Dillon had raised one brow at me as he finished up his cereal and then shook his head.

Apparently, I had just missed her. By literal minutes.

She had run out of the bedroom, grabbed all her clothes, had an awkward run-in with Dillon in the living room, and then had found her ride share so she could leave me without a word.

Not unlike what I'd done to her all those years ago.

Damn it.

I still couldn't quite believe what we had done.

Yes, we had done it before, we had been with each other before, but it was still a little shocking to me that we actually did it again. I had loved being with Violet before, had enjoyed every single part of us. But I had truly thought that what we had was gone. Then, somehow, last night, she had turned to me, and I had done the same with her. I wouldn't regret it, because if I did, it would make what we did wrong. And it wasn't.

But it still made me want to punch something.

Because I knew it was all a mistake. I had known it was a

mistake going in, not because anything with Violet would be bad, but because it wasn't the right time. She had said that she was taking advantage of me, but I still felt like I was the one taking advantage of her.

Maybe I deserved everything I got, because I seemed to be making one mistake after another—just like I had before.

But I couldn't focus on that, couldn't concentrate on Violet right then. Because I had to focus on the issue that was the bar.

I was starting to hate Connollys, little by little, day by day. It had been a touchstone for Jack and Rose. It had been their place. Something that had kept a roof over their heads and kept them together. They had loved working here, and they had brought us in when we were just kids, freshly out of whatever other foster home or street we had been in or on at the time.

They hadn't cared that, yes, they worked at a bar and owned one, and had brought in children during working hours. We had never gone behind the bar, at least not then, but we had still seen how the business worked.

We had seen how it ran correctly. The place had been thriving back then, with constant regulars coming in and out. There had been other bars around, but this place had been the hopping one. Maybe that was because of Jack and Rose. They had been that good, that amazing.

Or maybe it was because the other places around here weren't quite as good and they closed before Jack's did.

I let out a breath, trying not to focus on that last thought. Because I didn't want this place to close. It was mine, Aiden's, and Brendon's. And as I looked over at my youngest brother, I thought it might be Dillon's, too. No, Dillon's name wasn't on the deed, and he wasn't going to lose anything if this place closed, but he was still my brother, our brother, and trying to figure out how all of that worked within these walls was a whole other matter.

"What's up with you?" Brendon asked, his brows lowered. "You're not even out there working, yet you're glowering."

"You only think I should glower when I'm out there?" I asked, annoyed that Brendon had walked in on me in the back office. I just needed time to get my thoughts in order, and the fact that that's what I kept doing these days was starting to piss me off.

"I don't even get you. But we have a problem."

I leveled my gaze at him, really hating that statement. "That's not the first time you said that. What the fuck's going on now?"

"Well, the printer that we used to get the word out, as well as the publicity team that I hired to help with the online stuff got the date wrong."

I shook my head. "Huh?"

"For wing night. You know, the whole day that was supposed to bring in new people and new flair with Aiden's wings and his other new stuff on the menu? It's not going to happen today."

I froze, trying to comprehend what my brother was saying. "What do you mean it's not going to happen today? We've been working on getting this ready for the past month. I had to make sure that the place looked nice, but it always does because Beckham and I know what the fuck we're doing. Aiden has been working on getting that new menu ready, including two new types of wings. We've been getting *everything* ready for today. Your job was to get people in. And you're saying you didn't get it done?"

Brendon raked his hands through his hair, looking the angriest I had ever seen him. And I had seen Brendon looking pretty mad.

"I don't fucking understand it. I've used these people before, but they totally fucked up this time. If it weren't for the fact that I know they're not working with another bar, I would assume they were trying to sabotage us. But it's simple human error. I just didn't catch it."

I pinched the bridge of my nose. "And why didn't you catch it?"

Brendon turned on his heel and threw his hands up into the air. "Because I have another job. Because I'm doing this on the side of what's actually bringing in money. And because I'm stupid. I don't know. I'm sorry. We're just going to have to figure out what to do with tonight because it's just not going to happen the way we want it to."

"We're going to lose a lot of money on this. You get that, don't you?"

"I am the money man. Yeah, I get that. And you can yell

at me, punch me, do whatever the fuck you want. But don't worry about it, because anything you do, I'm going to want to do more to myself. I'm never working with that company again. I'll just have to do that all on my own from now on."

I folded my hands over my chest, anger coursing through me. Not directly at Brendon, but he was in front of me, and that meant he got the brunt of it. "You say that, but I'm thinking that maybe we should be helping you out there because you doing it on your own clearly isn't working."

Brendon froze and stared at me. "Seriously? You're just going to kick me out, just like that?"

"Didn't say that. But you had one job and, apparently, you're not doing it right."

"That's the problem. I have more than one job. We're all floundering here, and I don't know what to do with this place. Nothing that works for my other businesses is working on this."

"Because that's the food service industry," Aiden said as he stormed into the office. "And you know how the food service industry is. Yes, you're a brilliant businessman, but you know that food service is completely different than anything else."

"Yeah, that's why I try not to dip my toes into those waters."

"Well, you're already dipped. You've done a whole dunk into the damn thing. We grew up here, Brendon." I started pacing the office, anger rising in my chest. "Why can't we get this right? We're not fucking idiots."

"Yeah, well, doesn't seem the case right now," Aiden muttered under his breath, and I turned on him.

"Just stop it. This is getting frustrating. We're trying little things, trying to bring this place up, but the problem is that people just don't come in here anymore. They go to the other four hundred places that are within walking distance."

"Maybe we can get one of those apps and do takeout orders or something?" Brendon muttered under his breath, starting to take notes on his phone. "Or try different ways to get people coming in like another wing night."

I knew Brendon wasn't talking to me, just brainstorming ideas off the top of his head, but it was still frustrating. "I don't want to close this place, but we're not working together, and it's fucking us over. Don't you get that?" I rubbed my hand on my shoulder and continued to pace.

"Well, of course, we're not working together. We don't even like each other." Aiden shook his head and leaned against the door frame.

"I don't *not* like you guys," I said, my voice low.

"Yeah, that's not really a ringing endorsement," Brendon said, smoothly. "I happen to like both of you, you're my fucking brothers. I'm the only one out of the three of us, no, make that four of us, who's not blood-related to you guys, but I actually like you. I want to make sure that this family doesn't blow up. We are a fucking family, and we're not doing anything about it. Yeah, you ran away, Cameron, because you had things to do, but you didn't come back until now. You didn't come to us when you needed us."

I stared at Brendon, wondering where this had come from, and at the same time knowing it was probably overdue.

"I tried to come to both of you. You ignored me."

"Because I was angry with you, but then you never answered my calls either."

"I just can't, I can't with either of you," I grumbled and tried to catch my breath.

"Then why don't you just leave?" Aiden snapped. "You're very good at that. That much I can remember. So just leave. Go home and find another place to work. If you hate it here so much, then just go."

I rolled on my twin, wondering what the fuck had happened. Because this wasn't just me. This wasn't about me leaving to go take care of Dillon. This was something more, and I didn't get it. But I didn't know how to ask Aiden because I knew that my twin wouldn't answer anyway.

Maybe there were just some things that blood couldn't fix.

"I can go," Dillon said from the doorway. I hadn't even known the little asshole was there, and now I was afraid that somehow Dillon had heard too much, even though we hadn't even mentioned him. Not really.

"What?" I asked, confused.

"If me being here is screwing everything up, I can go. I have friends. I can find somewhere to stay." The kid raised his chin, and I knew that it was taking everything within him to actually say the words.

"You're not going anywhere. You're part of this, too."

Aiden flinched ever so slightly, and I wanted to punch the asshole. Didn't Aiden see that Dillon needed people? That Dillon was one of us?

Then I paused, wondering if I saw it. Because none of us were actually talking to one another. We were talking over each other, fighting about what we couldn't fix. Arguing over something that wasn't there anymore.

Brendon started yelling, saying something about numbers that made no sense to me. Oh, it probably would have made sense if I were actually listening, but I was focused on looking at Aiden and the way he was *not* looking at Dillon.

What the fuck were we doing?

Why couldn't we just talk and work this out?

Then I remembered living on the street when we were younger, holding Aiden close because we were so scared and didn't know where we were going to get our next meal. I remembered going from one home to another, trying not to get beat up by one of the foster dads, or touched by one of the foster moms—or another foster dad.

I remembered being stripped from Aiden's arms, screaming and reaching out to him even as he reached out to me.

I remembered wondering when I would see my brother again—if at all.

I remembered eating a worm out of the dirt one day

when I was so hungry I couldn't stand it, and that was the only thing I could think of to do.

I remembered finally seeing my brother again after so long, when really it had only been about a year or so—maybe even less. I hadn't been able to count the days because I wasn't able to go to school like I should have.

I hadn't seen a calendar or known exactly how many hours had passed since I last saw my brother.

But over the years I was away from him again, I knew exactly how many days had passed. How many months.

I knew because I had helped put that distance between us.

And I didn't know how to put us back together again.

Because it wasn't just me anymore. It was Dillon. Dillon deserved to know Aiden. He deserved to have a future. Yes, both of us had screwed up because we didn't know what we were doing in terms of this whole growing-up thing. But we were learning it together. I just never thought that I would be learning it with only the two of us and not with my other brothers.

I needed to fix that. Because this was fracturing. It wasn't the walls of the bar cracking, it wasn't the fact that the business was failing.

It was us. We were.

And we wouldn't be able to fix anything else until we fixed ourselves.

But with the way Aiden's jaw was set, and the way Brendon kept pacing back to his phone as if he were doing two thousand things at once and not able to focus on what was in front of him, I knew that today wasn't going to be that day. So, I let out a breath and nodded at Dillon so the two of us could leave.

"You always leave," Aiden shouted at my back. "That's what you're good at."

I stopped where I was, knowing that if I said anything in the mood I was in, I would fuck things up again. But I couldn't help it. Fucking things up is what I was good at.

"At least I was fucking there for him. You weren't. You didn't have the balls to even try."

Aiden looked like I had punched him. And maybe I had in a way.

Brendon finally looked up from his phone, his eyes wide, his jaw a little slack.

And then I turned on my heel and walked away again, putting my hand on Dillon's shoulder so he knew that he wasn't alone.

I'd come back to the bar later and work my shift, but that's all it was. A job. I didn't feel like this place was mine. Didn't feel like this place was anyone's, really.

We were going to lose it because we couldn't figure out what to do with each other, let alone the business.

And, yes, that was ignorant and probably stupid.

But there were some wounds you couldn't heal. There were some things you just couldn't fix. And as I thought about the woman who had been in my bed this morning, I realized that maybe that was true for more than just my family, more than just this business.

Maybe it was true for everything I touched.

Maybe I just couldn't fix anything because I wasn't worth fixing.

CHAPTER ELEVEN

I wish I could strangle your brain sometimes. Out of love. Because screw migraines.

- Allison in a text to Violet

VIOLET

THERE WAS a special place in hell for overhead lighting, the sunlight that was streaming through my open curtains, and any form of light on any electronic device I owned.

Yes, I was slowly losing my mind because of everyday things, such as light.

Let there be light, my ass.

Bile rose in my throat, and I staggered my way around

my living room, doing my best to keep my eyes shut as I drew my curtains closed.

When I decorated this house, I had known that I had a migraine issue. I'd had it since I was a teenager, and no amount of Botox shots or any other meds seemed to help. Oh, they would help for the short-term, but it was like my body got used to them, and then I would get another migraine the next month that would set me back even more.

So, I had made sure that I had beautiful curtains that looked decorative but were also able to block out any form of light that could come at me.

So, while sunlight was the thing of the devil, my blackout curtains were peace.

At least, part of that peace.

I rummaged around, trying to ignore every single sound that I was making since it seemed amplified right then, and found the scarves and other sheets that I used to cover my lampshades and other things around my house.

I still needed some light to function, but I could mute it as much as possible.

In the end, my house would resemble a den of iniquity, but I didn't care because, somehow, it gave me comfort.

Not that I was anywhere near comfortable just then, but I could at least try to improve my mood.

My stomach grumbled, and then I almost threw up, knowing that while I was hungry since I hadn't eaten in over a day, there was no way I could swallow anything. Just the idea of anything more than water—and water was a lot at this point—would be too much for me.

I had gotten home from Cameron's the day before and had fallen face-first onto the couch, groaning as my head started to ache.

I didn't even have time to think about the fact that my heart ached or that anything else a little lower ached, as well. I was too busy trying not to throw up on myself because everything hurt. Thankfully, I had fallen asleep, but I had done so with the curtains open and a single lamp on. That first burst of light into my eyes when I opened them after my very horrible rest had been too much for me, and I had thrown up right on my carpet.

I was usually better at preparing myself, but I was so out of sorts from everything that had happened, that I was clearly too many steps behind on this migraine.

"I just want to go to bed," I whispered to myself, but then I winced because I had been far too loud. Even a whisper was too much.

Everything seemed like it was too much.

I staggered around my house again, finishing up the clean-up on my rug. I had started it before and then had gotten nauseous and had to take care of my stomach again before I could finish cleaning.

Doing anything while suffering from a migraine hurt, and it was almost too much to bear, but cleaning up after yourself because you got sick because you were in pain? That was one of the worst things.

Thankfully, it was still the weekend, and I didn't have to work until tomorrow. But I really didn't know if I was going to be up for even that. Though it wasn't like I could just call in sick and say that I would try to catch up.

I already had to catch up on work that I had been a little slow on because I was so in my head when it came to Allison.

And Cameron. But I wasn't going to think about him.

I couldn't.

Regardless, I felt like I was losing my wits and everything else because I was just not up to being the Violet that I needed to be.

Just thinking about the fact that I had to work tomorrow not only made me nauseous again but also reminded me that I didn't know when or if I was going to get my next set of grants. With the random shutdowns that kept happening in the government, I knew that my funding was going to come to a close soon.

So, I was making sure that I had backup plans in place when it came to working with the university. Though I didn't want to only teach. Yes, I liked it while I was doing it, but I really enjoyed the research side more.

But there wasn't a lot of money for me to keep doing it these days. There wasn't enough money for any of us.

And on that depressing thought, I put my hands over my eyes and laid down on the couch again.

The house smelled of cleaning products and my own

stench that I really didn't want to think about. But I didn't even want to take a shower, just the thought of the action was too much for me. My skin hurt. Everything hurt. My *hair* hurt.

I didn't even know that it was possible for someone's hair to hurt this much, but here I was.

Everything just hurt.

And because I needed to be in the middle of the house just in case I had to get water or rush to the restroom or do just about anything other than sleep and pretend that everything was fine, that meant I had to stay in the living room.

I hated whining, but that's all I could really do with a migraine.

It wasn't just a simple little headache like the media might have you think. People that said, "oh, no, I'm getting a migraine. This really hurts," really didn't understand that sometimes that was just a headache.

And, yes, headaches were horrible, and they sucked, but they were nothing like a debilitating migraine.

I'd had them for most of my life, and I was still trying to figure out exactly how to get through them.

I remembered the last time I'd had one of the worst ones ever. I had been down in Colorado Springs, supposed to be watching my brother's daughter, Daisy. Daisy had gotten sick herself, and my brother hadn't been answering his phone. That meant that I had to call his—at the time—ex-girlfriend to come and pick Daisy up and take her to the hospital. Thankfully, Adrienne had rushed to help, and she had been on all the call sheets for Daisy at the doctor already.

And, even more thankfully, Adrienne and Mace were now together, happy, and getting married.

At one point, I used to think that I maybe helped in that a little, but I didn't really want to rely on my migraines to keep my family happily in love.

And now I was losing my mind because that's where my thoughts had gone.

I was just about to fall asleep again when there was a soft tap at the door. I wanted to groan.

Maybe it was the UPS man with my latest Amazon shipment. It didn't matter that I had a Prime addiction, Amazon was my everything. Of course, I didn't remember Prime shopping, but that was the deal with Amazon. Sometimes, you just opened your door and there was a package that you had forgotten you ordered.

I just lay there, hoping that whoever it was would go away, but then there was the sound of a key in the door and the lock turning.

There were only a few people with keys to my house—my parents, Mace, Sienna, Harmony, and my neighbor, Meadow.

The latter, it seemed, was who it was, because she walked in, tiptoeing inside the house with a frown on her face. I forced one eye open so I could get a good look at her, wondering why she was here.

"I'm sorry, I watched you staggering into the house yesterday, and I haven't actually seen anyone moving inside since," Meadow said softly as she came closer. And it was then that I realized that she had a whole box of things with her, and it wasn't from Amazon.

No, Meadow wasn't a good friend, but she was a friend nonetheless. I didn't really know her all that well, other than the fact that she was always there for me when I was having a bad migraine. Meadow worked from home, and her office window faced my house. And because she actually liked light—while I hated it today—that meant that, sometimes, she couldn't help but notice when I came home or left.

I remembered that Meadow wrote textbooks or something, or maybe she edited them. She also tutored when she wasn't working on those. I couldn't imagine reading right now, all I wanted to do was go back to bed. Or throw up. Or maybe try for some water. Nope. That just made me want to vomit again.

"Hi," I croaked. Keeping my eyes closed.

"I just wanted to drop off some things in case you're ready to eat later. And I figured I'd clean up around here as quietly as I could if you needed me. Then, if you need to wash your hair or do anything else, I'm here for you."

Meadow started puttering around, and I held back a smile. Not because I didn't want to smile, but because that action would probably hurt. Everything hurt.

Meadow was about my age, gorgeous, and single. I didn't know why she didn't have someone special, other than the fact that maybe she just didn't meet many people because she never left her house.

Of course, not leaving the house would probably be a nice thing because I didn't want to leave my house just then. Every time I did, I had to deal with more drama. Situations that I put myself into, I remembered.

No, my work drama really wasn't my fault. Neither was the fact that Lynn was there and had been texting me all weekend.

I'd ignored most of them because I had been sleeping, but she kept wanting to check in on me, making sure that everything was fine with our working relationship.

It was all a little too much, and I couldn't focus on anything. So, I wasn't going to focus on any of it at all.

I was just going to pray that this migraine would be over soon.

I felt someone move closer to me, and I opened my eyes to see Meadow sitting on the coffee table, looking at me.

"This is a bad one?" she asked, keeping her voice low. I was grateful for that.

"Yeah," I whispered. I used to try to nod or shake my head and answer so I wouldn't have to talk, but I figured out that doing that hurt more than just the whisper.

Migraines were the work of the devil, that much I was sure.

"Is there anything you need?"

"I don't know. Death?" I froze as soon as I said the words, and Meadow did, too.

Meadow didn't really know my other friends, but she had met them a few times over the past few years. She hadn't been at Allison's funeral because she had been out of town for something, but she had sent flowers. She also knew exactly how Allison had died, and she had been by my house to help me after the migraine that had come from me reliving exactly how I found Allison.

I didn't realize how much I used the word *death* in random conversation. Didn't comprehend that I said stupid things in the vernacular that hurt even more.

But it wasn't like I could apologize to Meadow for making myself hurt.

So, I just let out a sigh and wrapped my fingers around the edge of the blanket, pulling it closer to me.

"I'm going to get a cool washrag so you can wash your face. You're sweating a bit, and I know that you don't like that on your skin."

"Everything hurts," I said. I wasn't just talking about my physical body either.

There was something in Meadow's eyes that told me that she understood exactly what I was saying. "I know."

She tucked me in a little bit more and then went back to my guest bathroom to get a washrag.

As soon as she came back and wiped my face, I let out a groan. It felt so good, as if maybe she could wipe away some of the migraine itself.

I knew it didn't make any sense because the rubbing, even as softly as she was doing it, started to hurt my skin, but the coolness made me feel like maybe I had a fever. I knew that wasn't the case, but migraines just knocked all of my senses out of whack.

"I know you're not going to want to eat and the idea of it probably makes you want to get sick right now, but I'm going to put something in the Crock-Pot for you, and then I'm going to come by and check it later. I'm only doing that because you have nothing in your fridge.

"Shopping hurts." I paused. "That's not what I meant to say, but words hurt." She snorted, and I held back a smile only because that, indeed, would not be the least painful thing I could do just then.

"I know everything hurts. But you're going to have something to eat later for yourself that will last the whole week, or I can freeze it for you. Either way, it will be food. For later. But for now, just try to keep down some water and go to bed. I'm here if you need me."

"Thank you, Meadow."

"You'd do the same for me."

I really wished that was the truth. And maybe it was. Because I knew I would do this for Harmony and Sienna. And, yes, I would probably do the same for Meadow, she just never seemed to need me. I was always the needy one. But all of that just reminded me that I had not been there for Allison when she needed me. Needed us. She hadn't asked for help, but I hadn't seen that she needed help either.

Was this survivor's guilt? Or was this just the idea that

nothing was under my control and everything was just crumbling into pieces.

I didn't know how long Meadow had been there, but when the doorbell rang, I let out a scream. Well, at least a silent scream. I put my hands over my ears and rocked back and forth.

Who was the evil person on the other side of that door? Who would dare ring the doorbell on today of all days?

Meadow was still apparently in my house because she padded towards the front door then opened it and whispered something fiercely.

I couldn't make out the words, but as soon as I heard the deep tones of a whisper on the other side of the door, I knew exactly who was at my house.

Of course, he was here.

Meadow, ironically, knew everything about Cameron because we had gotten drunk on wine and cheese one night when we first started hanging out at my house, and I had told her everything. From the fact that I had loved him, to the fact that he had left me.

Then, we had held each other's hair back as we threw up because we'd had one too many bottles of wine and one too many bites of really stinky but amazing cheese.

So that meant that Meadow knew exactly who Cameron was as he walked into the house.

Then, the traitorous bitch left me.

Okay, that was uncalled for, but I was in pain, and she

was out of the house after quickly waving goodbye and leaving me alone with him.

Cameron.

What was I supposed to do? I was helpless here, and all I wanted to do was crawl under the blanket and never find my way out.

"Those damn migraines," Cameron whispered, his voice low. Cameron had seen me during a migraine or two back when we were dating, but I'd hidden most of them from him, mostly because it hurt too much to deal with human beings.

But he had helped me through a few of them, and he apparently remembered exactly what to do. He went and got another cool washrag, the best thing ever in the history of the world, and then somehow got himself onto the couch with my head on his lap.

He ran his hands through my hair, softly petting me back to sleep.

Nothing had ever felt so good.

And nothing would ever feel this good again.

This was perfection.

I slowly drifted off to sleep, without him even saying a word. Because, honestly, there was nothing he could say to make this better. There was nothing he could say that I would want to hear.

All I wanted was to get better. Somehow, with my head on Cameron's lap and his hands in my hair, I knew that just might happen.

That probably should've scared me, but I was so warm and comfortable right then, it didn't.

Nothing else mattered.

CHAPTER TWELVE

CAMERON

VIOLET WAS ON MY DICK.

That was the only thing that kept going through my mind as I watched her finally fall asleep as she lay on my lap, my fingers playing with her hair.

Violet was on my dick.

And not in a good way.

I let out a soft breath, trying not to shift because I knew that might hurt her, and then she would wake up and feel like crap even more.

I hated seeing her in pain, and these migraines were no joke. They had always been debilitating and seemed to knock her back a few steps. I hadn't known how to help her back when we were younger, and I still felt so far out of my depth that it wasn't even funny.

I remembered back when we were first dating, and she'd gotten the start of a migraine in front of me. She had tried to hide it. At first, I didn't know if it was because someone had made fun of her for them, or if she was just embarrassed or proud, but I'd been really confused.

I had always thought that migraines were just more painful headaches where you could just pop a few pills and get through it.

I had been wrong. Seriously wrong.

I'd held back her hair when she threw up, and I had learned how to take care of her using cold compresses and by just lightly running my hands through her hair.

She'd always told me that she hated being touched when she was in pain, but me running my fingers over her scalp had always felt good.

So, I did my thing. I massaged Violet's scalp, and she didn't back away. Finally, she slept.

It was odd that even after all this time, I could do these things, and she could just relax in my arms. So, here she was again, asleep on my lap, very close to my dick, and finally looking like maybe she was at peace.

And, yes, there was something deeply wrong with me for thinking about my dick at a time like this, but I couldn't help it, she was Violet, and my thoughts tended to stray there more often than not with her.

It was late in the day, and I had worked the afternoon shift at the bar. I didn't have to go in tonight because Beckham was working. I could have if I wanted to, just to check things out and maybe actually have a conversation with my brothers, but I had come to Violet's instead because I had texted her and she hadn't responded.

That might make me needy, but I had actually started to get worried. Because even when we were angry with each other back in the day, she'd always texted me back. She always let me know that she was okay. And she hadn't this time. I hadn't heard from her at all since she left my house, and Dillon had been the last person I knew that had spoken to her at all. For all I knew, she hadn't gotten home safely, and something was wrong. I had even texted Sienna to ask if she knew whether Violet was okay, and she had said that she hadn't heard from her sister all day either.

I had not only worried Sienna and therefore Harmony, but I had started to worry even more myself.

So, I had driven over here to make sure that she was okay, only to find that she was anything but.

I was grateful that her neighbor Meadow had been here for her, and from the scents coming from the kitchen, the other woman had made dinner for if and when Violet woke up and was actually in the mood to eat.

I didn't know Meadow, but she had let me into the house just fine, so I guess she trusted me or had at least heard of me. Or Meadow was a serial killer, and I had just let her out of the house after she had tried to murder Violet but had gotten interrupted.

I pinched the bridge of my nose. I really needed some

sleep if I was going on about that in my head. Yep, I was losing my damn mind. But that wasn't anything new.

Violet shifted ever so slightly, her hand under the blanket I'd pulled over both of us slowly rubbing along my inner thigh. I froze, making sure she was still asleep before shifting myself so she wouldn't accidentally touch something that would probably make both of us uncomfortable.

Thankfully, she went right back to sleep, and I just lay there, making sure I kept my fingers on her scalp, trying to ease away the tension of the migraine.

I had no idea what it felt like to actually have one, but I was glad about that. From the way they literally took Violet down to the ground and made it so she couldn't do anything but try to breathe, I knew I would probably react even worse than she did.

Because she had an inner strength that I was a little jealous of. And because I was one of those guys who actually reacted like the joke of a guy with a man-cold said we did, I probably wouldn't do well with a migraine.

With the temperature in the room, and the sweet smells of whatever Meadow had put in that Crock-Pot drifting over me, my eyes slowly closed, and I found myself falling asleep even though I hadn't meant to.

Violet was out on my lap, and I laid my head on the back of the couch, telling myself that I wouldn't sleep, that I would just rest for a little bit.

. . .

I SNORED myself awake at the sound of my phone buzzing.

I held back a curse and slowly reached into my pocket to pull it out, very thankful that it hadn't woken Violet.

She was hopefully on the other side of her migraine if the vibrations against her head hadn't sent her into another tizzy.

Hell, that probably wouldn't have felt good at all if she were awake.

But she was still sleeping, snoring slightly.

I thought it was pretty damn cute, and then I realized that there was no more light coming from behind the blackout curtains. The tiny sliver that I could sometimes see that told me exactly what time of day it was was no longer there at all.

I cursed again, this time a little bit louder as I looked at the clock.

Yeah, it was almost midnight, and that meant that I had stayed here for far longer than I wanted to.

I hadn't been sleeping well, thinking about Violet, the kid, my brothers, and the bar. Apparently, I just needed to pass out. It seemed Violet was the same way from the way she hadn't moved an inch from my lap.

The buzz of my phone was a text from Dillon, asking where the hell I was.

I couldn't really blame him, considering that I hadn't told anyone where I was going, and I sort of just lit out of the bar after my shift was over. I knew that Dillon was supposed to work the dinner shift busing tables and working on possibly starting to wait tables too, but I didn't even know what time he was getting off that day. That was Beckham's choice.

I let out a breath, then quickly texted Dillon back, telling him that I wouldn't be home but that I was okay.

Dillon: *You at Violet's?*

Me: *Yeah, she's not feeling well. You okay?*

Dillon: *I'm fine. Sorry she's sick. You need anything?*

And this is why I loved that kid. Not just because he was my brother, but because he actually cared about others. Yeah, he had that veneer of a perpetual teenager that was just on the cusp of adulthood, and he still acted like a brat sometimes, but he was a good kid. Somehow, Mom hadn't fucked him up completely. Hell, somehow our mother hadn't fucked Aiden or me up either.

I ignored the little clutch I felt at the thought of Aiden's name, knowing that I needed to fix things with my twin. Because my brothers were worth more than me walking away when things got tough.

But that was something for another day.

Today was about making sure that I didn't fuck things up with Violet. After all, she was the one still in my lap.

Me: *Everything's good here. I'm just going to make sure she's fine. I'll be home in the morning. Do you need anything?*

Dillon: *I'm fine. Worked. Going to play games. Eat. Sleep.*

I snorted. Yep, that sounded like any other night. Dillon hadn't made a bunch of friends yet in Denver, though I hoped that would change soon. I didn't really know how adults made friends, so I wasn't very good at it other than work friends and my brothers. But maybe Dillon needed to find a group of people to hang out with. Or he would do better once he was in school and could actually make friends among his classmates.

I knew when Dillon had said that he would just leave and go hang out with his friends so as not to bother my brothers and me, that he was talking about his friends from California. Those friends were off in college, and we weren't in California anymore.

I needed to do better about my little brother. Hell, I needed to do better about all my brothers.

And I would. Just as soon as I figured out what the fuck the right decision was.

Me: *Don't stay up too late. We have a morning shift.*

Dillon: *Well, I guess you do too. Don't stay up too late with your girl.*

I didn't say she wasn't my girl because it wasn't like I could actually say that now, was it? We weren't going to be able to ignore each other. Not anymore. And I didn't want to ignore her. Maybe that made me a masochist, knowing that it would hurt more in the end if things went to shit, but I didn't want to walk away. Not again. I just hoped that she would be able to forgive me. Because I missed her. I missed her so damn much.

Me: *Get some sleep. Thanks for checking in.*

Dillon: *I was just worried I'd have to go live with Brendon or Aiden or something if you croaked on me.*

I laughed this time, trying to quiet myself so I wouldn't wake up Violet.

Me: *Yes, that's what I'm going to do from now on. Every time you annoy me, I'll just threaten you with having to live with one of them. I've done it, it's not pretty.*

Dillon: *Yeah, cause living with you is such a joy.*

I could practically hear Dillon rolling his eyes. But I still smiled.

Me: *Well, I guess I need to threaten Brendon and Aiden with you then, don't I?*

Dillon: *** (middle finger emoji) ***

Me: *Goodnight, loser.*

I paused.

Me: *Love you, kid.*

There was no answer for so long, I figured he'd either not seen it yet or was just sitting there wondering what the fuck was going on. I didn't really talk about my feelings all that much, and I knew I needed to do better about that.

Dillon: *You too, bro.*

Something warmed inside me, and I hoped that maybe we were going down the right track. I loved that kid. He wasn't my actual son, but I had raised him, at least these last few years.

I didn't know exactly what Dillon had gone through, but I figured it was enough to connect us in some ways.

Now I just needed to find a way to connect Dillon and Aiden. I had a feeling that Dillon and Brendon would be just fine. I had watched them over the past month or so as they circled around each other. They didn't have the animosity towards one another as Aiden had for Dillon, even though Brendon hadn't known that Dillon existed either. It was more that Brendon and Dillon didn't really know how to act around one another and were being cautious. But there was no hatred.

I was really afraid that there *was* hatred when it came to Aiden and Dillon.

But that was on me. And I was going to fix it.

As soon as I fixed everything with the woman currently lying on my dick.

And on that thought, I slowly slid out from under her, grateful that she was still sleeping. I leaned down and ran my thumb along her cheekbone. And then I kissed her forehead. When she didn't wake up, I knew that she needed the sleep. I also knew that she probably needed a better place to sleep than her couch. Because, yeah, I loved this damn couch and how deep it was so it could fit both of us quite nicely, but I knew that she might like to wake up in her bed.

I slid my hand under her neck, and then my other arm under her legs and picked her up.

She snuggled into me, letting out a soft moan, and I willed my dick not to get hard. Because I loved that moan. She moaned like that often for me. At least she used to.

I tucked her into bed, wiping her hair from her face.

And then I put a glass of water by the bed, her migraine meds that I found in the bathroom right by it. I didn't know if she would need them or if we had missed the window for it, but I also didn't want to wake her up. Because when she was sleeping, she wasn't in pain, and I was going to count that as a win. And then I went and cleaned up the living room just a bit before putting away the dinner in the Crock-Pot. Thankfully, Meadow had kept it on warm, and everything seemed just fine. But I still found some Tupperware in one of the cabinets and as quietly as I could, put everything away and did the dishes. I didn't know if the Crock-Pot was Meadow's or Violet's, but I figured that leaving the ceramic part in the drying rack with the rest of it on the counter was just fine.

I was exhausted, but I wasn't about to go sleep in bed next to Violet without her knowing that I was really there. Nor was I going into the guest room because that just felt weird.

I looked at the couch that I actually liked, took one of the throw blankets from the other end, and laid down, knowing that tonight might be slightly uncomfortable, but I'd be just fine.

I didn't want to leave her all alone. Didn't want to leave her at all. I had to figure out what exactly that meant, though.

I WOKE up to the feeling that I was being watched. And

when I opened my eyes, I smiled up at a very groggy-looking Violet.

She narrowed her eyes and pouted just a little. "Did you tuck me in?"

I stretched but kept my head firmly on the little throw pillow she had. "A couple times. You doing okay? What do you need?"

"I don't know. I just didn't expect to actually see you here. I kind of thought that you were just like part of my imagination and I had just wished you here or something."

I smiled. "You wished me here? Like you wanted me here?"

I didn't know why I sounded so needy, other than the fact that I was indeed a little needy.

"I don't know. But, I'm glad you're here. Thanks for taking care of me." She rubbed her temples, and I sat up quickly.

"What's wrong? Do you need anything?"

"I'm fine. I think. It's just coming out of a migraine. It hits me hard. It's sort of like waking up after a very long cold or when you sleep so hard that everything seems just...off. You know, like when you take a nap in the middle of the afternoon, and you wake up and realize that it's like that time right before dinner, but you feel like you've already slept and you don't really know if it's light or dark outside and you're a little off? That's how it feels, but like a little bit harder and a little bit longer."

I snorted.

"Seriously? Hard and long is going to make you think of a dick?" She paused and then laughed. "Okay, now that I'm saying it again, totally a dick."

I laughed, still keeping my voice pretty low. "Sorry, apparently, I resort to being a teenage boy when I first wake up."

She looked down at my crotch, and I snorted. Yes, I did indeed have morning wood. "Apparently, in more ways than one."

She rolled her eyes, but not as much as she might normally have, and I figured she was still probably right on the edge of feeling better from the migraine.

"Want me to make you some breakfast?"

She froze. "Really? You want to make me breakfast?"

I shrugged and then twisted on the couch so my feet were on the floor and she was standing in between my legs. I ran my hand along her hip, and she didn't pull back. I counted that as a win.

"If that's what you need. If you want something like toast, I can do that pretty easily. But I'm pretty good at breakfast. Or we can heat up some of that stroganoff that your friend made for you. Though I think you have to add the cream at the end. Which would make sense if she didn't want to overheat that."

"Meadow made stroganoff? I knew she said she made something in the Crock-Pot and I could smell something delicious, but I couldn't really put two things together and form an idea of what it could be."

"You always did like stroganoff."

"It's like one of my favorite things ever. Maybe I'll do that for lunch or dinner. And I need to thank Meadow for making it. And I'll thank you, too."

She leaned forward and kissed me softly. I didn't move or pull back. I just let it happen, worried that I'd scare her.

"Thank you," she said softly.

"You're welcome. I'm here for you, Violet. Always. Anything you need."

"I'm starting to really believe that."

She let out a shaky breath and then sat down on the coffee table in front of me. She rested her hands on my knees as if she needed to touch me but wasn't exactly sure what to do. So, I put my hands on the couch, gripping the edge slightly so I didn't move forward and scare her too much.

"Thank you for taking care of me. Thanks for just being here. I had forgotten what it felt like to have your fingers in my hair. It always made me feel safe. So, thank you for that. And just thank you in general."

"You're welcome."

"What are we doing?" she asked, and I blinked.

"I thought I was going to make you breakfast."

"No, I meant what are we doing. Everything is so complicated, Cameron. I'm afraid that if we continue to do this, we're just going to make it worse. Our lives are already so connected with how much time we're all spending together these days. What if we mess it up?"

"What if we don't?" I hadn't meant to ask that, but it really honestly seemed like the best thing to say.

"I don't know how I survived losing you the first time, and I don't want to do it again. So, we have to take this slow, or at least as slow as we're doing now." She winced, and I kind of winced along with her. "Yes, we've already had sex, and we might have sex again."

"Well, I'm going to be honest and say that I hope we do."

"Yeah, I kind of like the sex, too."

"Kind of?"

"Fine, it's the best sex ever. But let's get to the actual subject."

I tabled that, but I really liked the fact that she'd said, "best sex ever." Not going to lie, that also made my dick hard. "Okay. So, what are we going to do?"

"I don't know," she said softly.

"I didn't want to leave you before. But I did. And I can't take that back. But I'm here now. And we keep finding ourselves in each other's circles. I keep coming right back to you. And I think it's always been you. I'd like to spend more time with you. I just want to know what happens next. And I want to know what you think. And I want to just...I just want to know I'm not making a mistake. I like being with you. And I hope you like being with me."

I hated talking about feelings. Hated opening myself up like that. I wasn't really sure what else I could do right then, though. I just had to be honest. Because lying and walking away when things got tough is why everything got all messed up to begin with.

"I guess it's pretty complicated, but it makes sense. And I hated that you left. It hurt. But I'm not that person anymore. We're not that young. So, if this doesn't work out, we both have to tell each other. You can't walk away again. And I can't walk away just to hurt you."

She paused, and I just sat there, waiting to see what she would say next.

"I'm going to have to forgive you. And I guess I have to forgive myself for thinking that was the end, too. That it was the only thing that made me who I was."

"You were always more than just me, Violet. I hope you know that."

"It took me a while to figure that out. But I did. And I guess...I guess this means we try."

I nodded hesitantly. "We try. And I'd like to take you out sometime. A real date. Where we get to know the Violet and Cameron we are now. And we try to figure out what the next step is. Because I wanna take that step with you, it's just figuring out what that is that's the hard part."

She laughed. "Figuring out the next step is the hardest part of every phase of life. But I guess I'm going to figure that out with you. Because I can't stay away from you, Cameron. Even if it might not be the best thing for me."

I leaned forward and kissed her hard, surprising both of us. "I guess it's my job then to make you see that it's not a mistake."

And then I kissed her again, hoping that we weren't making that mistake. Because I wanted her in my life. And that meant I had to be a better man than I was and make sure that she saw that I wasn't the guy that would walk away again.

And that meant I had to fix everything else in my life, as well.

Because Violet deserved more than a man with a failing business and a family that was falling apart. And hell, so did I.

I guess that meant that this conversation was going to be the first of many for me.

But now, I had Violet in my arms, and that was a pretty good way to start the morning.

CHAPTER THIRTEEN

The outdoors are evil. Why must you love them?

- Allison in a text to Violet

VIOLET

GOING on a date was supposed to be nice. Going on a hiking date could be very cute. Going on a hiking date where I actually had to work and collect some samples wasn't really my best idea, but between both of our jobs, Cameron and I had been a little too busy to do anything about this new relationship of ours.

I pressed my hand to my stomach, trying to keep my breath steady.

New relationship. I still didn't know exactly how that had come to be. One moment, I was having a headache of a lifetime and trying not to throw up again, and the next, I was sitting in front of Cameron, and we were discussing who we were as one and the fact that we could actually try and make this work.

I had been so hurt when he left, felt so broken, but he knew that. He knew that, and he had apologized. He'd apologized, explained, and even groveled.

I couldn't hate him anymore for what he had done. Because we all made mistakes, some of us more than others, but there had to be a reason for forgiveness. If not, what was the point of an apology at all?

"Are you regretting asking me to come?" Cameron asked as we walked to the back of the SUV where all of my equipment was.

"What?"

He leaned forward, cupped my face with his hand, and ran his thumb along my jaw. I loved it when he touched me. And he was doing it more often lately. In the past week since we both decided to try this whole romance thing, and even though we hadn't seen each other much, he kept touching me. It was as if some new switch had been flipped in both of us and we were just trying to figure out who we were. But he wasn't holding anything back. At least it didn't feel like it. He had even kissed me right in front of his brothers when I stopped by the bar after work a couple of days ago. I'd only been able to stay for ten minutes, but he had still kissed me. Much to the pleasure of his brothers, who had hooted and hollered.

"I asked you if it's really okay that I'm here. I was a little worried that you were going to regret that I came along."

I blinked, trying to focus on the here and now rather than the eight hundred thoughts twirling in my head. Sometimes, it felt like more than that, and sometimes, all I could do was look at Cameron and just think of one thing.

Him.

Yes, I was officially losing it.

"I'm sorry, just thinking. But I am glad you're here. Even though this is a very weird date."

His eyes narrowed even though I could see the laughter in them. "Are you saying that I'm the weird date? I mean, you are the one dating me. So, I guess that makes you weird, too."

"Oh, shush. And yes, you are weird. Very, very weird. But I like you anyway. Despite all of that."

With one hand still on my face, he wrapped the other arm around my body and patted me on the ass. "Okay, I'll be your weird date. But only because you're weird, too."

"Yes, because that makes total sense."

"I try. Now, I'm here, and I'm the one with the big muscles." He paused, using his hand that had been on my face to flex his muscles for me. That meant he still had his other hand on my ass, but I didn't think he minded. I didn't. Remember that part where I was losing my mind? Still doing it.

"Yes, you are all muscly and pretty. But I am still very muscly myself." I flexed both of my arms and waggled my brows

"I know. I've seen you naked.

"Okay, we're going way off track here." I rubbed my temples, trying to force my mind to focus on what I actually had to do today. Technically, I was working, but it was for the project that I'd already been paid for, and it was side-work. I had already collected most of my samples, but I wanted to gather one more. I didn't really need Cameron here to lift anything since I could do it on my own just fine, but it was nice not to be alone. Plus, the whole idea of being alone in the woods after listening to way too many true crime podcasts where a woman alone in the woods ended up murdered didn't seem like a great idea.

"You don't have to lift anything. I can handle it."

"I know you can handle it, but I'm here. That means you don't have to handle everything on your own."

For some reason, I had a feeling that those words had more to do with everything about the two of us and not just what I needed to get out of the back of the SUV. But I wasn't going to touch that, not then.

"Okay, then you take the really heavy bag with all my equipment in it. But that stuff is more expensive than anything you own most likely, so if you break it, you buy it. And since I don't think you can actually buy it, I'll have to take your soul." I lowered my voice. "And it's been a while since I've had a soul."

Cameron started laughing just like I wanted him to, and I grinned. I wasn't usually this dorky, this weird. But Cameron seemed to bring it out of me. It was like I could just be myself in strange ways like I had been before everything changed.

Yes, I was still worried about work and the fact that Lynn hadn't even wanted to be on this trip with me today. I was still worried about how my sister and Harmony were doing because none of us were truly finding ways to heal. And I was still worried about Allison. No, worried wasn't a good word for that. I was just broken over it.

But I was going to figure it all out.

"Tell me where you want me," Cameron said, and I smiled.

"You have to stop saying things like that, or I'm going to get all nervous and say something stupid. Or more stupid. Or is it stupider? You know, for someone who has a Ph.D., I really suck at grammar sometimes."

Cameron shrugged and picked up the bag that I knew was heavy, but with those muscles of his, he could handle it. "I think the English language just makes it hard for anyone to actually know. The I before E, except after C thing. Totally a crock. Because there's a whole list of words that make that a lie."

"You know, it's kind of sexy when you talk about grammar and the ways that it sucks."

"Don't get me started on those letters that don't actually

say anything. I mean, this is how you spell it, but the P is silent? Never made any sense to me."

"Well, I'm sure we could rant about it on social media, but that's probably already been done. Like a thousand times."

"True." He paused, then took a deep breath. I looked at him, wondering how this had happened. How the two of us had actually come to be here after everything changed. But then again, time passed, and people changed. And that meant that who we were to each other was changing, as well. Hopefully, it would be for the better. "It's gorgeous out here," he said, his voice sounding a bit odd.

"And it's my job to try and protect it."

"I know, it can't be easy. Humans are kind of the worst thing that's ever happened to Earth."

"Don't even get me started. I literally wrote my dissertation on that."

"But you'll find a way. All of you. Because that's what you do. You find a way to protect all of us. But, damn, I've missed this place. Yes, California was gorgeous, and I loved the ocean, but apparently, I'm a mountain man. Because look at this."

He moved his free hand around to gesture at the big mountains and plains all around us. "This is stunning. And, somehow, this is real. I mean, you look at pictures of it, and it looks beautiful, but then you sit here, and it doesn't even look real. It looks more real in photos than it does when you're actually focusing on it in real life. Like I could put my hand on that tree right now, and it wouldn't feel like it was truly here." He paused. "Okay, now it sounds like I'm eating some of those mushrooms that are probably around this forest."

I laughed, shaking my head as the two of us went down the trail. "No, it sounds like you're in awe of this place. I am, too. That's why I'm here to save it. Or at least try. I'm focusing more on the streams and tributaries right now than the rest of it. The others on my team are focusing on the other types of eco-life. But my grant was for water, so I'm going to take a few samples, and then we should be done. It shouldn't take too long."

"Just tell me what to do so I don't fuck up your science." He brushed his free hand down my arm, and I looked up at him, smiling. "I love when you get all science-y. You're brilliant, Violet. Just hope I remember to say that more often."

I blushed, ducking my head. "You're not so bad yourself."

I knew I was smart. I always had been, and I was never really ashamed of it. But it was still a little hard to call myself that. And it was really hard to sit there and not act like a schoolgirl and giggle when Cameron said it to me as plainly as he had. It was just one of those things. Maybe it was part of my self-consciousness, but I would find a way to deal with it. I always did.

We walked down the trail, talking about things that didn't matter, and some things that did. The sun was shining, and there was a slight breeze. It was always a little colder when you got closer to the mountains so, thankfully, we were both wearing light jackets. It didn't take long to collect the samples, and I knew I could have done this on my own, but it was kind of nice spending the day with Cameron.

"The guys don't mind that you're out here today?" I asked as we made our way back.

He shrugged. "I'm working tonight, and this way, it gives the three of us a little more breathing room."

I winced. "Things aren't working out all that well right now?"

"Things are pretty much sucking, but we'll figure it out."

"Are you talking about the bar itself or your brothers?" I had waited to ask more about this because I wasn't sure I would be privy to the knowledge. After all, Cameron and I hadn't really been dating all that long, and I didn't want to pry when it wasn't my business. But now we were a couple. Now, we were trying to figure out what exactly we were to each other and move in a new direction that neither of us really knew anything about. And that meant I needed to know his fears, his wants, and his desires. I needed to know if he was dealing with anything in his life that was hurting him. Because, somehow, I wanted to find a way to fix it. Or at least be there for him. He had been there for me so many times since he came back from California. Now, it was my turn to try and help. Hopefully.

"A little bit of both." He shook his head as I reached to help him with the bag when we got back to the SUV. We were the only people in the small lot that really wasn't a lot. It was behind a gate for no trespassing, but I was allowed in here with my grant. Meaning, no one would be around if we wanted to talk about something that Cameron didn't want to be overheard saying. "I've got it."

"Okay. Now, do you want to tell me exactly what you mean by that?"

"The fact that I've got it? Yeah, let's talk about the bag itself." He put my equipment in the back of the SUV and shook his head. "Do I have anything else? Not really. Yes, well, I'm not really going to touch on the fact that you and I are trying to figure out who we are. Because that...that's something that we're working on together. As for my brothers and the bar? I have no idea. We're trying to save Jack's place. It's just not easy when I don't think the three of us really know what we want to do with it. And a lot of it's out of our hands. A lot of it has to do with the fact that it is the food service industry and it's not easy."

"And I guess you have to deal with the fact that you guys really haven't been in the same place for long, at least not at the same time." I was trying to dip my toes into the waters and not cause waves, but I wanted to help. I really loved the Connolly brothers, and I hated seeing them hurting.

"I'm not a hundred percent sure what we're doing. But that's pretty much been the case for a while now. The three of us—four of us if you include Dillon and, frankly, we need to include Dillon—are trying to figure it out. I'm just not good about doing that all the time."

I reached out and squeezed his hand, and he gave me a small smile before continuing.

"Aiden and I fucked each other up. But we were always like that. It was mostly to do with our mom at first, and the fact that I went to Mom because of some misguided notion that she needed me. That hurt him. And I know it's not the case, but I have a feeling that he thought I chose her over him. Hell, it's not just a feeling, he told me straight to my face that's how he felt. I was an asshole, a real big asshole."

"But you also wanted to help your mom. And then you had Dillon."

"I did. And I'm never going to regret going out to California. I can't." He looked at me, and I nodded, swallowing hard. "I will always regret how I handled getting there. Hurting you? Dumbest mistake of my fucking life. And I'm never going to truly forgive myself for that. And I shouldn't."

"But we're moving on from that," I said firmly. "Because we have to."

"And that's something I know that you are far too gracious about. But, thank you." He kissed me hard and then continued. "But I fucked it up with Aiden, and Brendon, too. That much I know. I'm trying to fix it, I just don't know exactly how to do it. We need to sit down and talk, but we're too busy yelling at each other most times to actually get it done. And then there's the whole elephant in the room. Dillon himself."

"Because he's not a little kid anymore. He's a man, even if eighteen doesn't feel old enough to be a man."

Cameron snorted. "Don't I know it. That kid can vote and fight and die for our country, but I still want to wrap him up in bubble wrap and make sure that nothing harms him. And at the same time, I want to kick his ass because we keep making stupid mistakes."

"You sound like a big brother, maybe even a little bit like a dad." I whispered that last part, having not really meant to say it.

"We do have this weird relationship. And we're working it out. Dillon's a good kid. Or man, I guess. But we're figuring it out. It's just not easy sometimes when we're constantly butting heads with each other, yet still trying to be on the same side when it comes to Aiden and Brendon. Because I hate the fact that there are sides at all."

"If there's anything I can do, just let me know. I hate seeing you guys hurting like this."

"I hate seeing it, too. And we're going to fix it. Because there's no other option, damn it. Dillon's my brother, but so are Aiden and Brendon. The four of us will just have to find a way to be a happy fucking family. And if I knew how to do that, we would already have it in the bag. So, just one thing at a fucking time." He shook his head, and I smiled at him, going on my tiptoes to kiss his jaw.

"You're pretty amazing, Cameron Connolly. I just hope you know that."

"Yeah? How amazing am I?"

His hands reached around and grabbed my ass again, bringing me close to him. So close, in fact, I could feel the hard line of his erection pressing into my belly through his jeans and my shirt.

"Cameron Connolly, are you thinking what I think you're thinking?"

"You know it could probably ease all my hurts if you just kept kissing me. You know, kiss me to make it better."

"First, that's a low blow. Second, I have a feeling that you're not actually talking about kissing your lips."

He grinned and looked down at his crotch. I laughed. "Cameron."

"You told me yourself that no one would be here. Why don't we steam up the windows like we used to?"

"Really? That's your line? Steaming up the windows?" I pressed my thighs together because it was indeed a very damn good line.

"What?" he asked, acting all innocent. There was nothing innocent about him, and that's how I liked it.

"Fine. I will have sex with you in the car. But we're using the back seat and not the front one like we did that one time because I hit the horn with my back, remember? And then we woke up that dog that started barking, and then we were afraid that the cops were going to come. It was a whole thing."

He started laughing and then picked me up quickly. I wrapped my legs around his waist and kissed him.

"I was kidding. We don't actually have to have sex out here."

I smacked him on the back of the head softly. "No, no, I

want you right now. And you're the one who teased me. So, we're going to be very gentle so that we don't hurt the car."

"Hurt the car?"

"Or anything inside the car. We're not kids anymore."

"Yeah, I am pretty old. I don't think my back's going to be able to take it."

"So, I'll be gentle. Now, get me into that car and let's do it."

"Ah, yes, so sweet. Very innocent."

"You're the one who started all of this."

"No, you did. Just by being you."

I ignored the way that my heart clutched just a little. I still didn't know exactly what the two of us were doing, but I was really enjoying this part. I enjoyed how it made me feel all warm like there wasn't anything hard in the world that we couldn't handle.

Because it wasn't easy, and it never had been. Cameron had always had shadows, and I hadn't always known how to help. Sleeping with Cameron wasn't going to fix everything, it wasn't going to make everything better, but sex was never easy either. It was a connection, and it meant something to us.

Plus, I had missed him. And I liked the way we were now. So, even though I was looking into the past, I was also looking at the present and to the future.

And then I let all of those thoughts move out of my brain as he kissed me, this time deeply, and seriously.

"If you're sure," he whispered against my lips.

"With you? Totally."

He smiled and kissed me again. Somehow, the two of us got into the back of the car, my jeans down to my knees, his as well, though it hadn't been easy to get there. His mouth was on my breast, my shirt completely off, and my bra on the floor behind the driver's seat. He hovered over me, his dick covered in a condom, slowly working in and out of me as we moaned. It was soft, sweet, and still a little awkward since we were indeed in the back of an SUV, and Cameron was not a small man.

I couldn't exactly wrap my legs around him since we hadn't bothered to take off our shoes, but I still arched into him, running my hands down his back, sweat making it slick and easy for me to pull him closer.

And when I came, he came with me, and everything felt like maybe this could work.

Because, yes, we had made mistakes, and we would probably make more of them, but we were learning more about each other every day. Learning who we were. And we were taking those steps together. It was hard to trust, hard to truly believe that nothing was going to happen again in the future that might hurt me, hurt us. But I didn't think he'd leave me again, not like he had. We had both made promises that if this didn't work out, we would walk away together, but both of our eyes would be wide-open the whole time.

And I had to trust in that. Because if I didn't, then what was the point of this?

As he kissed me again, slowly working me to my peak

once more even though he had already finished, I knew that this was a different Cameron than the one I had fallen in love with before. Then again, I was a different Violet.

We weren't the people we were, and maybe that was good. Because those people had been unsure, and they had been hurt. I just hoped that the people we had become didn't hurt each other in the end.

When he kissed me again, and we cleaned each other up, I smiled at him, hoping against all hope that this could work. Because I had fallen in love with Cameron Connolly once before, and he had shattered me into a million pieces.

And I knew if I let myself love him again, it would hurt worse to lose him.

Then again, it could feel even better while I had him.

And that was the hope I clung to.

That was the hope that made me think that this could actually work.

CHAPTER FOURTEEN

CAMERON

TONIGHT WAS NOT GOING to suck. And if I kept telling myself that, it would actually go well. It was wing night part *deux*.

At least that's what Brendon kept calling it. I just kept thinking it was everything that we had hoped for all thrown into a bucket of doom.

Or maybe something a little more poetic, but I kind of sucked at the whole poetry thing.

That reminded me, I should probably send flowers or something to Violet. What did one do after you had some of the best sex of your life in the back of an SUV like you were teenagers rather than heading into your thirties?

There had to be a hallmark card for that. There was a

card for everything, maybe even a special flower. Nothing like red roses or anything. Maybe something purple. Was purple the color for car sex?

Oh, good. Come on, let's find me officially losing my damn mind.

Because there was no way my thoughts should be on random colors for car sex when tonight was wing night part *deux*, and I was afraid I was going to fuck everything up again.

Okay, not just me. The Connolly brothers were really good at fucking things up as a group. But I wasn't going to let that happen. I was not going to let our lack of communication and our issues with wanting to deal with the things that were actually right in front of us be a problem.

We were going to talk it out. We were going to make wing night work. And I was going to actually eat some bar food and enjoy life.

I was not going to let the business fail.

None of us were.

"You're looking a little green over there," Dillon said, his voice soft. Soft and yet there was still humor in it. That just made me smile, and I shook my head.

"Green?"

Dillon shrugged. "You know, nervous. I guess green's envious. Or maybe you ate the wings and are feeling a little nauseous?" He grinned as he said it, and we looked around the office, making sure no random customer had come to the back for some reason to overhear that.

"Shut your mouth. Don't let anyone else hear you joke about the food. The last thing we need is people not wanting the wings because of what you just said. And I'm not going to repeat what you just said because we're not going to let that happen."

"You really just confused me. But, anyway, you doing okay? Can I help?"

See? That was why I liked this kid. He may be slightly immature, may still need to figure out what he wanted to do with the rest of his life, but he was caring. He was not the product of our mother. He was just Dillon. And for that, I was grateful. I just wished that Aiden and Brendon could see it.

"Just nervous. Like always."

"Well, isn't your girl and the others coming? That should make you feel better." Dillon waggled his brows, and I just shook my head.

"Having Violet here will be nice, but three extra people eating wings won't really tip the bank scales. So, let's just cross our fingers that everything works out okay."

Dillon shrugged again. "There's a few people in, at least more than usual. I'm not quite sure since I haven't been here that long. Beckham's working, and I figured you'd be out there. They have me waiting tables tonight. Apparently, I'm training or something." He used his fingers to make air quotes when he said the word *training*, and I just shook my head.

"Yes, training. You need to learn how to work every part of the bar and restaurant."

I looked at him, frowning. "You're family, Dillon. When we were younger, we all learned every single part of this place. I always sucked at the cooking, but Aiden was damn good at it. Aiden hated working with people at the bar, but I liked that part. Brendon didn't like either but really liked working things from behind the scenes. So, let's see where you fit in." I paused. "That's if you want to. Fit in, that is."

Dillon shoved his hands into his pockets. "I don't know, man. It's not easy trying to figure out where I fit in, or if I will. And you know I hate actually talking about my feelings, so let's not actually talk about them, okay?"

I shook my head. "Today, we will not talk about your feelings if you don't want to. Mostly because you've got a thousand other things to do. But, soon, we'll be talking about it. Because, yes, we filled out the college forms, and hopefully you're going to get in, and everything'll be fine. But that's just gen-ed classes. What do you love to do? What's your passion?"

"If I knew that, I wouldn't be busing tables and possibly waiting on them."

"So, figure it out while you're in school. You have a couple of years or so of gen-ed classes, I would assume. Maybe start off in like the business sector or something? That should maybe give you the broadest options." And then I shook my head. "Brendon would probably know more about that, but he's helping you, right?" I knew that Brendon and Dillon had been talking more. I just didn't know what about since neither of them told me anything, and I didn't want to push. Well, now I was pushing.

"Yeah, he's helping. He read over my essays after you did and added a few more notes for me." Dillon held up his hands. "Not that you didn't help me out completely but, apparently, Brendon has a way with words or something."

I just smiled. "No, Brendon helped me with my school papers, too. He's a year older, remember? So, he had already gotten into college when Aiden and I were applying. He helped Jack and Rose and me figure out exactly what I needed to say. I'm glad he's helping you. He knows what he's doing." I paused again. "At least, usually. I think this bar is just stressing all of us the fuck out so much that we've all lost the ability to know exactly what we're supposed to be doing."

"You'll figure it out. You always do. You were really good at the place you owned back in California. And I know you made a shit-ton of money off it so you could come out here."

The kid grinned, and I rolled my eyes much like he did.

"It was not a shit-ton. But it was comfortable enough that I could help you with school. So, just don't fuck up. That way, I won't waste my money."

"I'll do my best. But no pressure or anything."

"Yeah. No pressure at all." I ruffled his hair like I had

done when he was a little kid, and he pulled back, laughing. That was when Aiden and Brendon walked into the office, their brows raised. Brendon looked like he was smiling, but Aiden looked like he had no idea what to do. That was something I would have to fix. I just didn't know how to do it.

"We ready?" I asked, rubbing the back of my neck. "At least, I hope we're ready, right?"

"We're ready. The printer and the publicity people that I worked with this time got the word out. And I know I said I was going to work on all of it myself, but that's just not feasible. I trusted different people this time, people that actually worked directly with me rather than against me. So, there are people coming in, and there better be some amazing wings."

Aiden shrugged. "Of course, there're good wings. And tapas. Because I don't really give a flying shit if you say tapas are too fancy. We're changing this place for the better, and yes, it's wing night, but we are not just some sports bar with no name and no ability to actually draw people in. It's going to be damn good food, and they're going to like it. They're going to come in for the gimmick, and then they're going to like the damn food, and then they'll come back. Because it's the only way we're going to make this happen."

My eyes widened at Aiden's words as much as the tone. "Okay, then. I guess I'd better get behind the bar."

Brendon shook his head quickly. "Before you do, there's a few things I want to go over."

"There're always a few things you want to go over," Aiden said, growling.

I noticed that Aiden glanced over at Dillon but didn't say anything. Dillon didn't say anything either. This wasn't a mess. This was a total fucking mess. But we were going to fix it one little wing and tapa at a time.

"Okay, I think the next step needs to be the pool league that we talked about."

I frowned. "Pool league? When did we talk about that?"

"He said it like on the second meeting you guys had," Dillon said, shoving his hands into his pockets just like Aiden had just done.

I looked over at the kid and nodded. "You really should be taking notes for us, like an executive assistant or something."

"Good thing you didn't call me a secretary, or I'd have to kick you in the shin," Dillon said.

I looked over at my other brothers, all of us with laughter in our eyes. Yes, this kid was pretty amazing. "Okay, so what is this about a pool league?" I asked, trying to remember exactly what we had talked about when I first moved back. I didn't really remember much since everything had been thrown at me all at once and it was a little confusing.

"It's a co-ed pool league. I've started talking with a few other bars about it. What it does, is we bring in teams from the surrounding bars and bring in a shitload of people, and you do about four couples per night playing pool. It brings in money for watching it, brings in money for the actual league itself. And we can make it a whole thing. We just need to make sure that we have the right people playing from our bar."

I nodded, going around the desk to make some notes. I pulled up my phone and started typing. "I remember now. I think we did something similar to this back in one of the bars I first worked at when I moved to California. My bar didn't actually have a pool table so we couldn't do that. But this could work. It could really work."

"Of course, it'll work. I've thought about it a lot. I ran all the numbers, and it can at least put us in the black for this quarter and into the next. Then, we can figure out the next step. But as soon as they come in and eat Aiden's food and taste our beer? It's going to work."

"Of course, my food's going to bring people in. I'm amazing." I knew Aiden was joking, but still, it was kind of nice having my twin actually like what he did for a living.

"And, Beck and I've been working with bringing in different beers for people to try. The ones from California, and maybe some others that may not be as famous but taste amazing. So, between what we have on tap and the food, we should be able to keep them here once we get them through the doors."

"Okay, let's make tonight work. The special starts for sure in about thirty minutes, but people are already starting to come in and order."

"Let's make it happen," I said, reaching out and putting

my hand on Brendon's shoulder. "We're going to make this work. We're not going to let Jack's place die."

I reached out and put my other hand on Aiden's shoulder. I knew this blocked out Dillon slightly, but I needed these two guys to understand what I needed them to do. "This place is part of us. We can't lose it. And we're going to make this work." I gave them both a squeeze and turned so I could let Dillon back into the circle. "The four of us can make this work."

I emphasized the word *four*, while Brendon nodded, smiling, Aiden jerked a bit.

I knew it had been minute, and probably hadn't even been intended as mean, but Dillon had seen it.

"Yeah, the four of us," Aiden said quickly, and that made me sigh. The knot of anger or frustration that always filled me released slightly because Aiden hadn't sounded worried or anxious about me adding Dillon to it. We just didn't know how to make this work. I had never heard of a family situation quite like ours, and making these kinds of connections wasn't easy. But we were going to do it. Because I wasn't going to let it happen any other way.

Brendon cleared his throat and then nodded to Dillon before the two of them walked out. I didn't know if they had planned it or if it was just that the two understood each other, but soon, Aiden and I were alone in the office, and things were about to get even more awkward.

"Thanks for including Dillon," I said quickly.

"Yeah, I can't really exclude him, can I?"

"Aiden."

"We have to work. Let me just deal with that first. I'm trying, Cameron. I just feel like everything came out of the blue, even though it shouldn't have. And that's not just on you, it's on me, too. But I just need a moment to breathe. So, just let it happen, okay? I don't hate the kid. I just don't know him."

"That's my fault."

"No, it's Mom's. And both of ours. But it's mostly Mom's. And that's what I have to deal with. So, let's just work tonight and make sure we don't lose this place. Because I think if we do, I think that's it. You know? There's no coming back from that."

"I know. I love this place. It saved us."

"So, I guess we should save it back. And I'll try not to be an asshole to the kid. Mostly because I don't like acting like an asshole. It just keeps coming out naturally, and it's starting to bother me."

I laughed. "We're twins. I'm an asshole, too."

"Yeah, but at least you're getting laid regularly. I'm an asshole with just my hand."

"You know you could fix that. I saw the way that you were looking at—"

"Nope. Not going there. Your girl, though, she walked in as soon as I came back to the office. She was just taking a seat with her other girls. So, go say hello to Violet, and then get back behind the bar, and serve everybody some really expensive beer."

"You know that's not how this works."

"Well, it's how it should. Just make us some money. Now, I'm going to go make the most amazing food in the history of food."

"You are weird."

"I know. But it's what draws in the ladies."

"You just said you weren't getting any."

"Stop throwing my words back in my face."

I laughed. Loving this. We sounded like we had in the past, like the brothers that we used to be before we quit talking because we were too afraid of what the answers would be if we asked too many questions.

Aiden seemed to come to the same realization, and he stopped laughing, his eyes growing slightly cooler but not as icy as they had been for the past few months.

Things weren't completely better, but they weren't worse either. They were going to change. We were going to find what we once had, even if it was a little banged up.

I had to believe in that.

Aiden lifted his chin, not in anger but as a goodbye, and then went back toward the kitchen.

I let out a breath, rolled my shoulders back, and went out to the front.

There were indeed more people here than usual.

I almost wept in relief.

Dillon was out training while he was busing, doing more things at once than I thought possible.

The tables were full, the bar was packed, and while I knew that Beckham needed my help, he waved me off for a minute, and I knew that he was giving me some time to say hello to Violet.

So, I went over to the table, kissed her hard on the mouth, waved at the other girls, and then left her blinking at me without even saying a word.

Hey, maybe this whole figuring myself out thing was working.

Because I had a girl that I had once loved and knew that I was falling in love with again, brothers who might be confusing as all get out but who were trying to find our connection again, and customers who wanted beer, wings, and even some of Aiden's tapas.

I worked harder than I had in years, and I loved it. The back of my shirt was sweaty, my feet hurt, and I had a slight headache from the noise in the bar, but it was amazing. We hadn't run out of wings, but we had come close. I only think that we stopped from running out because everything else on the menu was ordered to its full extent, as well. And that stuff hadn't been on sale or anything.

It was pretty amazing.

Violet and the others left pretty quickly after eating, not wanting to take the table. And while I was grateful they had done that, I missed her. She had leaned against the bar and kissed me goodbye as her sister and Harmony laughed and waved on their way out.

It was just like it used to be, where we were a unit. Yet it was completely different at the same time.

Things were finally starting to die down, and Beckham waved me off, wanting to close part of the bar down like he always did. The man was super particular, even though he didn't own the place. He had his ways, and I wasn't going to stop him because they worked. Beckham was the best person we had, and I wasn't about to lose him.

I was just walking back to the office to see if there was anything I could do before I went back out to the front when I saw Brendon leaning against the doorway heading into the kitchen. I went up to him, about to ask what was wrong, when he held out a hand, quieting me.

"What?" I asked, my voice a whisper.

"Look," he said, his voice almost inaudible. He pointed over at Aiden, who was at the workstation fixing up a couple of tapas plates, and lo and behold, he wasn't alone.

Dillon stood next to him, wearing an apron with his hair back and gloves on.

"See, this is how you roll it," Aiden said, showing Dillon how to plate one of the appetizers.

I blinked, looking over at Brendon.

Well, then.

"Come on," Brendon said, pulling me back.

"How did that happen?" I asked as soon as we were out of earshot.

"I walked by, and Dillon went right up to Aiden and asked if he could show him how to do something back there."

"No shit?"

"No shit. Apparently, Dillon has bigger balls than any of us thought. Anyway, Aiden stood there for a second frowning with that normal glowering look that he gets and then he gave Dillon a tight nod and moved over so he could show him how to plate something. Never saw the kid's eyes light up the way they did at that."

"Yeah, I saw those eyes. I saw them once before when he was playing in that band of his. But even then, I don't think they were as bright as they were tonight. Shit. Maybe I should be looking into culinary school for the kid."

Brendon rubbed his chin, nodding. "Maybe. Let's get him into a couple of gen-ed classes first while he figures things out, and Aiden can help train him a bit to get his feet wet and see if that's what he likes. That is, as long as Aiden keeps playing nice. But I think he will."

"I think he will, too. I think we all have to."

"Let's just give him some time. I think time is what we all need, we just didn't really know what to do when we were waiting for that next step. You know?"

"I know. I miss you guys. Sorry I was a fucking idiot."

Brendon ran his hand through his hair, looking more disheveled than usual. The man never used to, but tonight may have been a busy night, and it meant more to all of us than just numbers.

"Aiden should have called. I should have called back. It's on us just like it was you. We were all just so angry with each other that it was easier to walk away than pretend that we had anything important to say. And so, yeah, I think Aiden and I lost out on a lot of time with a kid who's pretty amazing. But we aren't now. And I'm not going to take that for granted. And from what I just saw in there with Aiden? I don't think he's going to take it for granted either. So, let's just give him some time."

I swallowed hard, my throat feeling oddly full. I cleared it. "Time works." I paused again. "We'll work it out."

"We will. Because we're Connollys. And that kid in there? He's a Connolly too, even without the name. I don't have the blood, and I'm one. You and Aiden don't have the blood, and you're Connollys. So, Dillon is, too. He's one of us. And we're not going to fail him. We're not going to fail each other. Not again."

I didn't reach out and hug Brendon, even though some part of me wanted to. I just stood there awkwardly in the hallway, my throat thick as I waited for any shouts from the kitchen in case Dillon and Aiden stabbed each other or something.

I figured this was a good step in the right direction. We had worked hard. We had plans to get more people in, the food was amazing, the beer was fantastic, and I had my brothers back.

I just needed to keep them.

And along the way, I just needed to make sure I didn't

fuck up. Because I was good at that, and I was afraid that if I messed up again, that would be it. There'd be no coming back.

So, it was on me not to be the reason we lost it all.

And it was on me not to be the reason I lost Violet.

So, I would just have to do it. But the thing was, I wanted this. I wanted it all to be right. And I was going to do my best not to be the man I was before.

CHAPTER FIFTEEN

Shot! Shot! Shot!

- Allison in a text to Violet

VIOLET

"I THINK this was the best idea we ever had," Sienna said. I looked over at my sister.

Sienna had her head back on the chair, her eyes closed and covered by cucumber slices. I hadn't realized that some spas actually used cucumbers, but Sienna had apparently asked for them specifically.

I loved my sister, even if she was a dork. But then again, I was just as much of a dork as she was.

I didn't have the cucumbers on because they had slid off.

"It really was a great idea, Harmony," I added, sinking back into my chair.

My friend smiled, her eyes closed. "I occasionally have them. I knew we needed a day that was just us. We've been so busy with our various jobs and other household issues. Not to mention the fact that a certain friend of ours has a boyfriend, but I figured it would be nice to have some girl time."

"And thank you for inviting me, too," Meadow said, her voice soft.

"I'm glad you were able to come." I had invited Meadow to a couple of girl-time things, but this was the first time she had come to hang out with the three of us. I wasn't sure if it was because she actually wanted to hang out with us, or if it was the fact that she knew we were missing our fourth. Meadow wasn't replacing Allison, not in the slightest. Because we had always invited Meadow along with us even when we tried to do girl-time things with Allison. Meadow hadn't been able to come, but today, she was here.

And so, the four of us were enjoying our spa day, each of us in the middle of a different treatment. We were all completely clean, scrubbed, and massaged. I was going to get a facial soon, and I was contemplating getting a hair mask since the ends were getting a little dry these days. I had dyed it blond recently, and it was a little unhappy with me at the moment. But I liked the color, and so did Cameron.

A small smile played on my face, and I felt more than saw Harmony sit up and smile back.

"You're thinking of Cameron."

I looked up at her. "How on earth did you know that?"

"I see you didn't deny it."

"Of course, she's not going to deny it," Sienna said, her eyes still behind those cucumber slices. "Why would she deny it when she's getting laid?"

We all laughed, even Meadow.

"I think you're very lucky that we're behind closed doors right now or we'd probably get kicked out," Meadow said, a smile in her voice.

"As if they aren't used to a group of women talking about getting laid or random male body parts," Sienna said smoothly.

"Speaking of male body parts..." Harmony said, acting all too innocent.

"Hey, we're not talking about that. And, Harmony, I am truly shocked. *Shocked.* You are the sensible one of us."

"Hey!" Sienna said, finally pulling off her cucumber slices and setting them down on the table next to her. "I resemble that remark."

"I am the sensible one," Harmony said, throwing her hair back and looking very mysterious and classy. "However, I would also like to know about the size of your boyfriend's penis."

She said it so pompously that I couldn't help but snort.

Thankfully, I had already finished drinking my water, or I probably would've sprayed it all over everybody.

"You did not just ask that."

"I believe I did," Harmony said smugly.

"I too would like to hear about the size of Cameron's penis," Sienna added, not sounding quite as pompous but doing pretty well.

I scowled at both of them and then looked over at Meadow, who sat on my other side. "So? I take it you want to know, as well?"

Meadow raised her chin and then plucked at a non-existent spot on her robe. "I would never dare ask such a sensitive question. However, if that information was just casually mentioned, I would indeed take in any type of gossip you may have about a certain appendage of a man I might've just met."

I just looked at her, laughing. "You guys are sick. Sick, sick, sick."

They all laughed, and I just shook my head. I had missed this. Harmony had been right. We had been so focused on our jobs and just trying to heal after Allison that we hadn't taken time to just be together. It felt weird that Allison wasn't here with us, but it also felt strange that we weren't talking about her.

So, I needed to change that. Even if it hurt.

"You know who the first person would've been to ask about his penis?" I said, keeping my voice casual. We hadn't broached the subject of Allison, not in any real detail, but I didn't want to *not* talk about her. The more we pushed her down into our memories, the more I was afraid we were going to forget her. Or forget what she meant to us.

"Allison would've already known the size of his penis," Sienna said.

My brows rose. "Huh? Are you saying that she would've already seen it? Because I have questions about that."

Sienna shook her head, smiling, and this time I thought it actually reached her eyes. And we were talking about Allison. That was progress. Even if just a little. "No, I'm saying she would've already gotten it out of you. In fact, I'm a bit surprised that we don't actually know about the size and girth of this penis since you've already bounced on it a few times. In fact, you bounced on it a lot before. So, why didn't we ever ask before now? I feel like we're missing out on this whole friend thing."

"I agree. You didn't tell us about his penis at all before. Is there something we should know? Is his penis okay?" Harmony sounded so serious that I couldn't help but laugh, tears rolling down my face.

"I don't think we've ever actually used the word *penis* in conversation as much as we did just now."

"Oh, I think at my bachelorette party we said penis a lot. But we were drunk, and Allison kept saying 'shot, shot, shot.'"

Harmony laughed as she said it, and for that, I was grateful. We were learning, healing, and trying to figure out how to have conversations about the people who were no longer with us. We were not only talking about Allison, we were also talking about somebody's bachelorette party. A bachelorette party for a wedding to a husband that was no longer with us. That was progress. I hated that we had to have this kind of progress at all, but I didn't want to hide. I didn't want to be scared anymore. And I didn't want to feel this pain when I thought about the people who weren't here.

"Cameron's penis is just fine."

"I'm so sorry," Meadow said, deadpan.

"That's not what I meant."

"So, his penis isn't fine?" Sienna asked, leaning forward. "Is there anything you can do? Wait, he has to be really great at oral if his penis sucks. Because if he isn't good at any of that, I don't know why you're with him."

"Oh, stop it, all of you. Cameron's penis is amazing. It's long, it's thick, he knows exactly what to do with it. Oh, and he's really good at oral. He was really good at oral before, and he's even better now. I can come like three to eight times a night, just with that mouth of his. But his penis? Best penis ever. Now, I never want to have this conversation again because I think I'm beet-red. And I'm about to get some skincare that might be completely negated because we keep talking about the word *penis*."

They were all silent for a moment before everybody dissolved into fits of laughter. Soon, we were each wiping tears from our faces and shaking our heads.

"I'm so proud of you," Harmony said. "And so happy for you. I mean, a man that's good with his mouth and his cock?

It's like the holy grail." She paused. "Well, maybe not the holy grail, that seems kind of sacrilegious right there. But you know, it's like a unicorn. Yes, Cameron is a unicorn."

"Oh my God. Now I'm going to picture him with like a horn on his head. Or like one of those…remember that photo we saw of the guy in all purple with like his mane of random-colored hair, and he had the hooves on his hands so he was like cosplaying a unicorn?"

"Oh God, now I'm going to just picture Cameron like that all the time," Sienna said. "I mean, we're going to the bar later tonight, right? Or is that tomorrow? Why can I never remember what my schedule is without my phone in hand?"

"The pool league starts tomorrow," I answered.

"Okay, good. Because now that gives me time to find something with a unicorn for him to wear for us. He can be our mascot."

"You've officially lost your damned mind," I said, laughing again. "And now, if I picture Cameron dressed as a unicorn while having sex with him, I'm going to blame all of you. If that happens, a curse on your sex lives. A curse."

Meadow patted my leg. "You know, it's kind of mean to curse our sex lives when you're the only one having one."

"You know, Meadow," Harmony said, leaning forward again so she could meet Meadow's eyes. "I think you're my new best friend. Because I totally agree. You're not allowed to put a pox on all our sex houses."

"I cannot believe you just tried to use a Shakespeare

quote. About sex."

"It's Shakespeare. There's always weird sex in Shake-speare." Sienna frowned. "Right? I actually don't remember reading Shakespeare. I mostly remember that movie with Leonardo DiCaprio. He was so young then."

I shook my head and leaned back, closing my eyes as my friends talked about Leonardo DiCaprio then versus now. We were all in agreement that we really didn't like him now but had had such a crush on him in *The Man in the Iron Mask*. What was it with that sweet baby face of his and that long hair? It made no sense.

"Seriously, though, you're smiling again," Sienna said softly, and the others quieted down.

I looked down at my hands, wondering if that was true. It could be, I didn't really know how to explain happiness. I had been so stressed about so many things and focused on trying to just keep my head above water, that the idea of joy seemed almost farfetched.

"I feel like I could be happy," I said softly. "Mostly because I feel like I'm me again, just not the same me as I was before."

"You're never going to be the same person you were a week ago, even a day ago. So, you're definitely not the same person you were when you were with Cameron the first time," Harmony said softly. "And that's okay. You're not supposed to be the same person after things happen."

"He broke me." I hadn't meant to say the words, but then again, my friends knew. Meadow might not know as much, but she knew a lot. And she was here now, so I wasn't going to hide how I felt from her. There was no use in doing that. Plus, I knew she had secrets of her own, and I never wanted to pry. "He broke me into a million pieces. He made me feel like I wasn't good enough. That I did something wrong that made him run away."

"I never did get to throat-punch him," Sienna said softly.

That made me smile, but only for a moment. "He apologized, though. He explained, and I forgave him. I do forgive him. And, yes, while I can't forget—we're not supposed to forget what hurts us—it does make me more cautious. But I also can't walk into every part of our relationship wondering when he's going to leave me again. That's not healthy, and it would make being with him completely idiotic. You know?"

"I think he realized what he did wrong. You can tell that he's not the same person he was. And from what you said, and from how he acts, he never left to be malicious. He didn't leave because he didn't love you."

I rubbed at my chest, frowning. "No, he didn't love me enough. Or I didn't love what we had enough. Maybe he didn't trust me at all. But I can honestly say it doesn't matter now. Because that's done with. He's back. He apologized. He groveled."

"But did he grovel enough?" Sienna asked.

"I don't know. I don't know if it would be enough for anyone else, but I think he groveled enough for me, for us. Because I see the way he is with Dillon. I see how his relationship with Aiden and Brendon is forever changed and

how he was forced into a situation that he doesn't understand. He doesn't know how to fix it. His relationships or the
bar. And every time I tried to pull away from him after he
came back, I found myself coming right back to where I was.
In his life, and in his circle. Someone else might think that
I'm stupid for believing I can trust him again, but if I don't
let myself fall, even just for a moment, I'm afraid I'll be
standing on the outside looking in at my life forever. I'm
afraid I won't be able to feel again."

"I'm going to ask you something, and I want you to be
honest. And I want you to not hate me for asking," Harmony
said quickly.

"Okay," I said, a little worried.

"Are you with him because of what happened with
Allison?"

I froze, wondering where that had come from. But since
it was from Harmony, I knew there had to be a reason.
Harmony had done her best not to make any major life decisions after losing her husband, and she more than anyone
knew how the pain of losing someone you loved affected
your decision-making skills. And she had done it twofold.

"I'm not going to say it didn't play a part in it. But I'm
not with Cameron to feel. I know I didn't say that right. I'm
feeling with him, but he's not the only reason I am. I have
you guys, and I have a career that I love even though it
stresses me the fuck out."

"Even with Lynn and douchebag?" Sienna asked.

"Even with Lynn and douchebag. And, honestly, they

literally mean nothing to me. They annoy me because I have to deal with Lynn on a daily basis at work, but I can avoid her, and I can still love my job. I can still be stressed out about funding and the fact that sometimes my research just doesn't work out the way I want it to. All of that is just normal daily life. Lynn and douchebag mean nothing to me. But Cameron means something. He always has."

"And being with him makes you happy. I know it's hard to quantify what happiness means, but he is." Harmony looked down at her hands before shaking her head. "And I see the way he is around you. He's always loved you, and he always looked at you like you helped raise the sun and let it set again in the evening. And I know he hurt you, and you can forgive him and not forget, and that is perfectly fine. You guys are both different people now, and I know you're in a different relationship than you were before. Neither of you is going into this blind. And I'm so happy that you found that. Because you deserve it. You deserve so much happiness." She paused. "And I know that Allison would feel the same. Because we all deserve happiness. Even if we don't think we do."

I wiped away tears, leaning forward to grip her hand. Sienna scrambled from her chair to come and sit on the edge of Harmony's seat to get closer. I moved slightly and opened up my left hand and gestured Meadow forward. Meadow looked a little hesitant at first, but then came and sat on the edge of my chair. Then it was the four of us, just sitting in silence.

I didn't want Meadow to feel left out, but I knew she might be uncomfortable. However, this was the future. This was where we were.

And we had to figure out what to do with that.

"I'm never going to understand what happened. With Allison, I mean," I said quickly. "I'm never going to understand, but I don't think we're supposed to. But she's gone, and it changed us. And I still think those changes are evolving. And I know that we're going to find ourselves in situations where it hurts again, and we won't know what to do. So, I want you to know that I'm here. I wish that Allison had known I was there for her, or maybe it didn't matter because she couldn't reach out anyway. I don't know what went through her mind, but I want you to know that I love you guys." I squeezed Meadow's hand. "And I know you're new to us, Meadow, but we're here for you, too."

"Allison seemed like such a bright person. I'm sorry she's gone. But I'm really glad that you three are here. You're such a cohesive unit. And I'm glad that you have each other to lean on." Meadow squeezed my hand back, and I held back a sigh of relief.

The four of us sat there, talking about Allison, and then our conversation led into other things—our work, our lives. Even Cameron again.

And when we cleaned up and made our way back to our homes, I felt a little heavier and yet lighter at the same time. It was good to talk about Allison, to have her in our lives even though she wasn't really here. I didn't want to forget her. I didn't want to not feel that pain when I thought of her. Because feeling those emotions reminded me that she had been in pain. That she had needed someone. And that maybe she'd just needed an answer that we didn't have.

The tears fell again, and I brushed them away as I walked into my home. Crying was fine. It meant that I was feeling something. And I knew I couldn't be numb anymore.

It wasn't fair to anyone for me to stay numb.

When the doorbell rang, and I answered it, I knew it would be him. Not just because we had made plans for him to come over after my spa day, but because I knew I could rely on him. And maybe that was silly. Perhaps I was in for heartache. But I needed this. I needed to feel.

And so, I kissed Cameron. I leaned into him as he held me.

Because this was just one step, one breath. We were figuring out who we were with each moment and with each passing day. Yes, I missed my best friend. I missed her with everything that I had. And I hated that she wasn't here.

But I was here.

And so was Cameron.

And I couldn't add the quantifier that he was here *for now*. Because that wasn't fair to either of us. So, I was going to live in what we had and be part of this relationship.

I knew I was in love with him. Again. I was in love with Cameron Connolly, and I prayed I wouldn't break again.

Because I was afraid of what would be left over if I did.

CHAPTER SIXTEEN

CAMERON

"THIS IS TOTALLY GOING TO WORK," Dillon said, pacing in front of me.

I smiled. "Really? I'm so glad that you have all this confidence."

Dillon rolled his eyes. "Of course, I have confidence. I think I'm the only one that has any confidence in this family."

We both froze at that, and my eyes widened. Family. I was pretty sure that was the first time Dillon had ever said the word when it had to do with any of us.

"I mean...you know what I mean. I'll just go work or something."

I stood up from behind the desk where I was going over some last-minute details and went to reach out for him.

Thankfully, Dillon quit moving and just stood there, looking down at his shoes.

"Family works. We were a family before, Dillon, the two of us."

"Yeah. I guess."

I closed my eyes and let out a breath before squeezing Dillon's shoulder. "No, we weren't. We really, really weren't. We weren't really a family when Mom was there, but that wasn't just you. She lost custody of Aiden and me, too. She just wasn't really good at being a mom."

"I never really thought of her as one anyway."

Dillon's words hurt, and I knew the kid was in pain. But they weren't untrue, so I kept going. "Yeah, I never really did either. I don't know why I even called her Mom, I guess mostly because it was just habit."

I usually called Jack and Rose by their names these days, even though I sometimes slipped up and called them Mom and Dad. Or maybe it was the other way around. It was always just a mix of the two for me. Dad and Jack. Mom and Rose. They were both. And they were so much more.

"Didn't you call Jack and Rose, Mom and Dad? They adopted you, right?"

I nodded and pulled my hand back to stuff it into my pocket. "Yeah. I was better about calling them Mom and Dad when they were alive. I think when I left, I kind of just went back to calling them what I had when I first moved in. I don't really get it. But you know, family's complicated."

"No shit."

"I'd say watch your language, but I guess you're an adult now."

That made Dillon smile. "Fuck, yeah."

"Hey. I'm still your elder."

"Yeah, really old. Like super-elder. Like Gandalf."

"Call me that again, and I'll kick your ass."

"Well, that means you'd have to actually catch me. You're old and feeble."

"That's it, I'm going to kick your ass." I reached for him, but Dillon slid out of the way and ducked before running right into Brendon.

My suited-up brother raised his brows before shaking his head. And then he reached up to undo his tie. "Sorry I'm running late, work got in the way. But I'm here to play pool and kick ass and take names."

"Yeah, totally not happening. I'm going to win."

"I still don't know why I can't play," Dillon said, sounding a little bit like he was pouting but not as much as he used to.

"First, Cameron, there's no way you can beat me," Brendon said, smiling.

"Second, you need to work, Dillon. Plus, there's no way that you have the skills the rest of the Connolly brothers have."

"The rest?" Dillon asked quietly and then seemed to shake it off. "Anyway, I should go back to work."

Brendon winced, and Dillon scurried off to go and get his stuff ready for busing. I met Brendon's gaze.

"Too much, too soon?" I asked, my voice deceptively casual.

"Apparently. We'll get it right someday. I kind of like the kid. But there's no way he can beat us at pool."

"Damn straight."

"There's also no way that you can beat me at pool." Brendon took off his suit jacket and hung it up on the hanger that we kept on the back of the door.

"I have Violet on my side, and she's a pool shark. The two of us are going to kick ass."

"No, Harmony and I are going to win. We're going to beat all of you."

"You know what's going to end up happening, don't you?" I asked, clearing my throat.

"Aiden and Sienna are going to end up wiping the table with all of us. Yeah. That sounds likely."

"So, tonight though, we're all set up?" I asked as Brendon rolled up his shirt sleeves.

"I hope so. I just walked in, but the scents coming from Aiden's kitchen smell amazing. My mouth is watering. I know it could be the fact that I haven't really eaten since lunch and even then, that was a really shitty salad, but I digress. When are the girls getting here?"

I looked down at my phone. "They should be here any minute. I'm really glad they agreed to do this with us."

"I don't know if they're going to do the whole pool league, though, they do have lives outside of this bar."

"Don't I know it," I said, only grumbling slightly. I

hadn't really seen Violet much this week between my hours at the bar—we were actually starting to hop a little bit better—and the fact that she was just working longer hours, finishing up her research grant material. That, and she had spent more time with the girls than she had before, and I didn't fault her for that. I still didn't know how I could help her heal when it came to Allison, but I figured she and Sienna and Harmony were working it out some way.

"So, four teams are coming?" Brendon asked, looking down at his phone for his notes.

"Yeah, we're going to do the three of us this time because you're starting it off, and then another couple or duo from one of the other bars. We'll have another night here where it won't be all of us but more of the other bars, and then we'll move on to other venues. I think in three weeks we come back here. We have it all written out, right?"

"Yup, I've been working with the other bar owners, and they're excited about this, too. Anything that brings more money to all of us."

"It's sort of working with the enemy of my enemy thing," I said, only slightly teasing.

"These guys really aren't enemies. As much as I'd like to think so. We don't have a group clientele, at least they do. We're the ones on the lower end of the totem pole here. But it should bring in more money for all of us in the end. At least, that's what I hope."

"Okay, I guess it should get done. It is kind of weird that

we're selling our skills in order to get people to come in." I rubbed the back of my head as I said that.

"Yeah, but hopefully it will get more people in for the next set we host. We're just going to be ourselves, sell this bar, sell our souls a bit most likely, and then get what we need to get done."

"So, I guess you'd better get down there and do it," I said quickly.

Soon, Violet and I were walking past the kitchen, bringing Aiden with us as my brother grinned, holding a plate of tapas.

It was nice to see him smile.

"Are these for us?" I asked, reaching for one of the small, bite-sized things that looked like it had cauliflower on it. Maybe?

Aiden smacked my hand, and I winced.

"Do not touch that. That is not for you, that is for the girls. Well, at least Sienna."

"Ooh, really?" I made sure to overexaggerate my words, and Aiden rolled his eyes.

"Not like that. Sienna likes to munch on things while she plays, that way she can beat all of your asses. So, don't touch. These are not for you," he repeated.

"But they're for Sienna? Interesting." Brendon leered as he said it, and I grinned.

"You guys have way too much time on your hands if you're thinking about Sienna and me. That is so not going to happen, ever."

Aiden froze for a moment as he said it, and I looked up, only to see Sienna in the hallway, both she and Violet looking at the two of us with their eyes narrowed. Sienna, however, widened her eyes for a fraction of a second before she shrugged and walked over to us.

"Good to know, Connolly. I was worried you were going to fall in love with me and things would get awkward. But as long as you feed me, I will be fine." She popped whatever that cauliflower thing was into her mouth, grinned, and then sauntered her way back to the pool area.

"Food," Harmony said, clapping her hands in front of herself. "That wasn't awkward at all. Brendon? Let's go claim a cue because I refuse to lose to these girls. You cannot make me out to be the loser here. Okay?"

I was grateful that Harmony was the one to speak first because, yes, that had been awkward. Brendon held out his arm, and Harmony pushed him out of the way, laughing as the two of them walked side-by-side back to where the two pool tables were.

I just looked over at Aiden and then Violet and then let out a breath. "Okay, then. Game on."

I took a few steps forward, kissed Violet on the mouth, and smiled again. "It's good to see you. I missed your face."

"You say the sweetest things. I missed your face, too." And then she patted my cheek and reached around to pat my ass. "I also missed other things." We walked into the pool area, and the others looked over at us.

"Unicorn!" Sienna called out, and I stared at Violet.

"Unicorn?"

Her cheeks were bright red as she shook her head. "Don't ask. For the love of God, don't ask."

"Well, now I'm kind of worried. Unicorn? Is that some kinky thing you want me to do?"

All three girls started giggling, and I thought I'd lost my damn mind. I did not understand women, even if I loved them.

The way the pool tournament worked was that each of the couples played each other, at least for the night, and then there would be points tallied for the winner. The tournament would last for eight weeks, and then at the end, there would be a big pool of money for the winners, and hopefully a lot of money for the bars that hosted the matches. Since we were starting it and it had been our idea, or at least Brendon's, we had most of our people up and stacked at the front. Two of the bartenders from Sandy's down the street had offered to take part, too.

One was a man named Samson who glowered and didn't talk to anyone, and the other was Charlotte, who apparently liked to talk to everyone. She draped herself over Brendon and then Harmony, and then she flung herself at Aiden before coming over to me. I really, really didn't know what she was up to. Was she just this flirtatious because she wanted to be? That was fine, but I was very taken and wasn't about to get involved in that. But I had a feeling she was using her flirtations as a distraction.

Too bad we were better at ignoring her than she thought.

I wrapped my arms around Violet's waist and kissed her hard. "You ready for this?" I asked, my voice low.

"Of course, I am. We're going to kick their behinds."

"Behinds?"

"Asses. Sorry. I'll add more curses to my daily life."

I rolled my eyes, and then we went to it, first playing against Brendon and Harmony.

Somehow, we ended up stripes, even though I had a feeling Violet had been going for solids when she broke. But it didn't really matter. We were going to do this. We were going to win.

We did not win.

Brendon and Harmony kicked our asses, but it was fine, we could still end up third for the evening and rack up some points for ourselves. That meant we had to go against Samson and Charlotte, who had lost to Aiden and Sienna.

"I'm going to head to the bathroom before we start again, okay?" Violet kissed me hard and then ran off towards the restroom. I watched her walk, my eyes on her ass before I pulled them away and tried to focus on the fact that tonight was fun. Beckham and the waitresses and one of our spare bartenders were working their asses off with the full crowd. People came to watch and then would move in and out of the area to go eat something, watch something on TV, or just have a few drinks. I'd never seen the pub this busy, and if we kept this up with new ideas and really good people, beer, and food, we would make it.

I was just going to rack the balls when Charlotte came over to me, rubbing herself along my side. I narrowed my eyes and took a step back.

"What's up, Charlotte?"

She smiled at me, a seductive grin that did nothing for me other than sound about a thousand warning bells.

"Oh, just wondering what a big man like you is doing all alone with his balls."

Dear God. That had to be one of the worst lines I had ever heard, and I had said some pretty bad lines myself throughout my life. Recently, in fact.

"I'm sure you and Samson are going to be hard to beat. But Violet and I...we're a team."

Was that subtle enough? Maybe I should just rub myself all over Violet so Charlotte got the message. Charlotte moved even closer, and I took a step back. But she moved faster, rubbing herself all along my side again before going up on her tiptoes to bite my ear.

Oh, hell no.

"Oh, I'm going to have fun with you tonight," she whispered, her warm breath sending revulsion through me rather than shudders.

I pushed her away, but even as I did so, I looked up to see Violet standing there, her eyes wide. She didn't look hurt so much as angry. No, there was hurt there mixed with the anger. She looked between Charlotte and me and then just shook her head before spinning on her heel and storming out of the place.

Everything had moved so fast, I wasn't even sure that anyone else had seen it. No one else had been in the room other than Charlotte and me, but I hadn't realized that until it was too late.

It didn't matter that I had pushed Charlotte away, it didn't matter that I hadn't done anything wrong. To someone who already had trust issues when it came to me and how I had treated her in the past, this looked bad, seriously fucking bad.

"Why did Violet leave?" Brendon asked, worry on his face.

I shook my head in answer. "I'm out, Violet and I call it. I have to go back to her."

Harmony stepped in front of me, though, her hand out.

"Harmony, get out of my way," I growled.

"Don't bark at her like that," Brendon snapped.

I glared over at him before trying to move past Harmony again.

"I can handle it myself, Brendon. And you cannot handle Violet right now. She's angry and hurt."

"What?" I hadn't realized Harmony had seen what happened. Not that anything had happened, but still.

"I just saw the tail-end of it, and while I'm sure you thought nothing was wrong, Violet is allowed to react how she wants to. She's already a little tender. So, I'm going to go and help her figure this out. You join Brendon and figure out how to work things out between the two of you and finish the game. Do it for your bar. I will help Violet." Harmony cleared her throat. "And don't tell Sienna until she's done. Let her win. She needs this happiness." Then Harmony picked up her stuff and walked away, leaving me with Brendon.

What the hell?

What. The. Hell?

CHAPTER SEVENTEEN

You're my person

- Allison in a text to Violet

VIOLET

I SHOULD HAVE DONE something other than walking away. I should have screamed, I should have asked him something. I should have gone to that woman and tugged on her hair and beat the shit out of her.

I should have done anything other than walking away.

But that wasn't me. I wasn't good at confrontation. I walked away and thought through my options before I figured out what I needed to do next. I went through every scenario, and then I reacted. I hid inside myself, and I let the reactions come.

That was how I operated. I wasn't someone who could just go up to someone else and scream at them how I was feeling. The fact that I had ever done that with Cameron meant that he got under my skin in ways that no one else had or could.

I rubbed my chest, at the same time trying to will away the migraine that I knew was coming on.

It hurt so much.

Should I have left them like that, knowing that it could have been more if I hadn't been there? Or knowing that it could have been more even if I had been there the whole time.

None of it made any sense to me, but it wasn't like I knew what I was doing.

I walked away because I was scared. Scared of what I had seen. Scared by the fact that I had trusted, and it had screwed me over.

I should have stayed. I should have talked it out. I should have answered my damn phone when he called later.

But now it was the next morning, and I had done nothing. I had done nothing because I needed to think.

And that had been a mistake.

Because now I was alone, breaking all over again, and wondering if I had trusted too quickly. It didn't matter that Cameron probably hadn't done anything wrong. That wasn't the point.

It was the fact that I had trusted too quickly.

The fact that, for a brief moment, I had *known* that I had made a mistake in trusting.

And because of that, I didn't know if I could truly trust *myself*.

It was like I was peering through the fog, trying to figure out exactly what hurt and why I couldn't react the way I needed to. I knew there were things I needed to do. I knew that I needed to talk to Cameron. I needed to realize that everything had just been blown out of proportion and it was all just stupid. I knew all that.

It didn't make it easy to do. It was like I was two steps behind, watching my life fall apart before me and seeing the decisions that I needed to make yet wasn't able to make.

And this time, I knew it wasn't just a headache, it wasn't just a migraine.

My heart hurt, and my palms turned sweaty, and I felt like something was constricting my chest. As if there was a two-ton elephant—or however much they weighed—on my chest right then, making it hard to breathe. Everything hurt, and I felt like if I didn't make a decision, I was going to mess everything up. But if I *made* a decision, it might just get worse. I couldn't focus, couldn't take everything in. I couldn't breathe, couldn't do *anything*.

Was this anxiety? Was this an actual panic attack?

I tried to suck in a breath, only it didn't work, so I sat down in the middle of the floor of my living room and forced myself to breathe, forced myself to focus.

Sweat dripped down my temples, and I tried to just be. I needed to focus on my breathing, if I did, everything would be okay. It had to be.

Nothing was out of my hands completely. Nothing was entirely scary. Everything was going to be all right.

Cameron wasn't cheating on me, that much I knew. But it was just seeing him there, having that split-second moment of insecurity that had sent me into a tailspin. Because I was so afraid that if I was wrong, I would break, and I couldn't be like that anymore. I couldn't be that person.

And then I thought of Allison. And I thought of why. And I just...I couldn't think anymore.

Because I didn't know why Allison had done it. I didn't understand why she had left us all, and why we were all still here wondering why she wasn't with us. It didn't make any sense.

I had gone through a divorce, faced the fact that my husband had cheated on me, and I hadn't reacted like this. I knew I hadn't loved Kent the way I should, and that was on me. I had still been broken over Cameron, and yet I had gotten with Kent because I thought it was the only thing that I could do to try and heal.

And then he had proposed to me, and I said yes. It had been too fast and too wrong. I'd thought I'd gone down the right path, that I was doing what was expected of me even though my family didn't know him and I wasn't sure I loved him. And when he left me for Lynn, I had been angry, but I hadn't been broken.

Cameron had been the one to do that to me.

And I had been the one to do that to myself because I had trusted him back then.

So, trusting him now was hard, and yet seeing that woman all over him changed something inside of me. Something I didn't want to think about.

Because Cameron had never once cheated on me. That thought shouldn't have ever come into my mind, and yet when he left me before, when he walked away without a second glance, I had thought that maybe there was someone else.

And maybe there was. Perhaps there had been the idea of another woman. His mother.

Not in a creepy, weird way, but in the fact that he had left me for a connection that he hadn't been able to fix.

And I had forgiven him for that. But I didn't know how to put everything back together again.

Why had Allison done this?

I asked myself that question again, I knew it was all connected.

Because how was I supposed to know when enough was enough and when the pain was too much? What had I missed with my best friend? If she was hurting, why didn't we realize it, why couldn't we find the answers? Were there any answers? Why was she gone, while I was still here? Why was the pain inside of me so bright, and why did it burn so much when I was still here, and she wasn't?

I stood up on shaky legs and went to the bathroom, looking at my reflection in the mirror.

All of my makeup had run down my face, my black raccoon eyes staring back at me. I looked like I was dying inside. I had bright red cheeks and even brighter eyes, and I didn't recognize myself.

Was it because I missed my best friend? Or was it because I didn't know why she was gone? How could I be okay with being here, with being alive, when I didn't know why she was gone?

My head started to pound, and I knew I just needed to take my meds so I could function. It didn't feel like a full-on migraine, but even a partial one could incapacitate me for a time.

I opened my medicine cabinet door, pulled out my pills, and looked at the bottle. I looked at the number that was left. Shaking my head, I quickly took one and drank my glass of water before putting the bottle away.

Every time I looked at my pills, at *any* medicine, I thought of Allison. And that worried me. Not because I feared for my life, but because I hadn't seen the signs in her. And I didn't like the idea that we'd never get any answers.

I didn't like the idea that the answers were never going to be there. That I would never know if I could have changed something. Done something.

I was being selfish again, but right then, where everything felt as if it were falling apart again, maybe I needed to be a little selfish.

"I need help," I whispered.

That was the gist of it all. I needed help. I needed help, and I wasn't going to get it. Not standing here looking in the mirror, or even talking to my friends. I wasn't going to get it by worrying if Cameron was going to come after me, or if he was going to call again. I needed to talk to someone who could actually help me with trying to figure out what I had overlooked, and what was wrong with me. Why I missed Allison so much.

I just needed help.

So, I took a deep breath and went to get my phone.

I needed help.

And so, I called my brother. Mace would help. He would know who to call.

Because I missed my best friend. And I didn't want to lose Cameron or myself because I didn't know how to deal with all of that.

So, I asked for help.

CHAPTER EIGHTEEN

CAMERON

VIOLET WOULDN'T ANSWER my calls. Did she not trust me? I cursed.

Then again, I didn't know why I was even asking myself that question. Did I even deserve Violet's trust? That was the question that needed an answer. I sure as hell hoped the answer was yes, but what if I was wrong? What if I was so fucking wrong?

"Hey, Brendon and I wanted to talk to you. You okay, bro?" I shook myself out of my thoughts, knowing that I needed to call Violet again, that is if she would answer her fucking phone. Or I could go there. Everything would be okay. I just needed to talk to her.

"I'm fine. Let's go," I said, getting up from the desk. I'd been going over the numbers from the night before, even though Brendon had already done them, and I liked what I saw. I just wished everything else in my life was working out. So far, only the bar was doing well. Considering that was the one thing that hadn't been doing well recently, maybe I should count my blessings.

I didn't want to count those blessings. Well, not just them. I wanted to count Violet among them, too. And that meant I needed to talk with her.

I followed Dillon out of the office and into the bar. We hadn't opened yet, so it was just my brothers and Beckham behind the bar, cleaning glasses.

"What's up?" I asked, knowing my voice sounded a little on edge. Hell, I was on edge.

"You want to talk about it?" Brendon asked, playing with the condensation on his water glass.

"I'm fine." I ran my hand over my face, knowing I needed to shave soon but not caring. I just didn't care about anything right now except for fixing what I'd messed up.

"You're not fine. Just go talk with Violet." Aiden glowered at me, and I sighed.

"I'm going to. As soon as she answers her damn phone."

"Go to her house," Aiden said quickly.

"Doesn't that border on stalking?" I was only partly joking.

"Not if you just do it the once, and you guys are already dating," Dillon said quickly. We all looked at him, and he held up his hands. "I mean, don't break into her house or crawl in through her bedroom to stare at her when she's sleeping or anything."

"What the hell are you watching these days?" I asked. Dillon shook his head.

"It doesn't matter. All I'm saying is you're allowed to go to her house. Don't force your way in, but ask her what is going on. If she tells you that she never wants to speak to you again, after that, well, then you have your answer."

I looked at my little brother and frowned. "You're suddenly a font of knowledge. I'm a little worried about you."

Dillon blushed a bit, ducking his head, and I leaned forward, a little concerned. "Well, since you're all here, I should tell you that I'm going to be a font of more knowledge soon." He grinned and held up a piece of paper like he was showing off a good grade, and then I realized exactly what it was.

All thoughts of my other worries slid out of my head, and I couldn't help but smile widely, elation filling my veins, even if only for a moment. "You got in? You fucking got in?"

Brendon cheered with his water glass, and Aiden looked between all of us, smiling. Smiling was good. Smiling was not scowling.

"Yep, I got in to the University of Colorado at Denver for the spring. Which is great because I have no idea what I want to be when I grow up, but at least I'm going to be spending a lot of money to take classes."

"Don't worry about the money. Just get good grades and

pass. Then we can figure out what you want to be when you grow up later. Which is really weird to say because it took me a really long time to realize what I wanted to be when I grew up." I went around the bar and hugged the kid, and Beckham poured sodas for everyone except for Brendon, who stuck with his water.

"Aiden?" Dillon asked, his voice soft.

I froze, not wanting to interrupt the moment, but if Aiden hurt Dillon's feelings, I was going to get really pissy. I was already on edge, and I didn't want to hurt anybody because I was so pissed off at everything.

"What's up, Dillon?" Aiden asked, his voice calm. Calm was good. It wasn't being an asshole.

"Will you still help me with the whole food thing? Because I'd like to do it, I just don't want to get in your way, but I also don't want to try out for culinary school when I know next to nothing, and then realize I don't actually want to do it and waste everyone's time, you know?" Dillon had stuffed his hands into his pockets and said the words so quickly that I barely understood exactly what he was saying as he spoke.

Aiden was silent for a moment as he studied Dillon, and I held my breath, hoping that they weren't going to come to blows—if even verbally.

"Of course, I'm going to help you. You're my brother."

I swallowed hard, emotion clogging my throat. I wasn't going to cry, but it was damn close. Hell, I didn't think Aiden had ever used those words when it came to Dillon before, and from the look on the kid's face, he realized it, too.

Aiden cleared his throat and looked around at all of us. Brendon leaned back as if he had a feeling he knew what our brother was going to say. I had no fucking clue and was a little worried. Then again, I was always worried these days.

"Since we're getting everything out in the open here, I'm sorry, Dillon. I was an asshole. I'm an asshole for many reasons, but mainly because I made you feel like you weren't wanted. That was never the case. I just didn't know how to deal with the fact that I had this long-lost brother on top of the fact that Jack and Rose were gone, and Cameron was back. We'll figure things out. If you want to go to culinary school, I'll help you there too because I am probably the best chef in Denver." He winked when he said it, and I laughed, all my emotions warring with each other. Holy hell. "Shut the fuck up, Cameron. I am the best. However, if you want to be second-best, Dillon, I can help you."

"And when the student surpasses the master?" Dillon asked, and I snorted, glancing at Brendon, who grinned widely.

"He has you there, Aiden. Make sure you don't teach him too well."

Aiden flipped us all off. "If he ends up being the best chef in Denver, it'll be because I've retired, but then everyone will know that I *taught* the best chef in Denver. Anyway, you need help, I'm here for you. And I think I'm a little done with the whole brotherly love thing, but just know that I'm going to stick here. I'm not leaving and going to another place. I like this bar. I loved what Jack and Rose did with it, and I love what we're doing with it. So, you're stuck with me for the time being."

"Good to hear, because the bar's doing fucking fantastic, at least for that one night. We're not out of the woods yet, but I can actually see the light at the end of the tunnel."

Brendon cleared his throat and looked at all of us, and I leaned against the bar, waiting. Beckham was there, part of our conversation. He might not be family, but he was close enough now. He was helping keep the bar in the black, and that was all that mattered.

"We need to keep at it. We need to keep working our asses off, but we're going to be able to keep Jack and Rose's place, at least for the time being. So, let's keep at it, and let's just not fuck up."

"Hear, hear," I said, raising my soda glass. We all clinked glasses and took sips, and I shook my head.

"I don't want to lose this place. I *can't* lose this place. So, I'm here. For the long haul."

Aiden nodded. "All of us are. But the kid's going to be in school soon, so I guess we're going to have to deal with a new busser."

"Hey, I need spending money."

I nodded. "True, but you're still not getting a raise."

"But I may be a server soon. I mean, my training did go well." Dillon grinned, and I rolled my eyes just like he had a habit of doing. I had been doing it often. No wonder teenagers did it incessantly.

"Okay, so we're all in agreement," Brendon began. "We're going to make this place work, and we're going to kick ass. Dillon is going to school to take at least some gen-ed courses until he decides what direction he wants to take. He'll figure it out, and we'll be there for him. And, Cameron? You don't have to pay for all of it. We are Connollys. We take care of each other."

"I'm not really a Connolly, though," Dillon said quietly.

I cleared my throat again, meeting Dillon's gaze. I hoped he understood that I was being completely serious now. "Yeah, you are. If you want the name, we can get you the name, but no matter what, you're a Connolly. You're our brother."

Dillon looked like he was on the verge of crying, but then again, I thought the rest of us were, too. At some point during the conversation, Beckham had quietly walked out. While I appreciated it, I kind of felt like we were all in need of a beer or something, even if the kid wasn't old enough to drink and it was still a little bit early.

"While we're on the subject of brothers..." Aiden said softly. I stiffened and looked over.

"Yeah?"

My twin let out a breath. "Don't ever walk away again. We're brothers. I walked away, too. That much I know. Not answering your call for a fucking year? That's on me. I didn't deserve for you to ever call me again after that. You tried.

You even came here to my house to try and tell me about Dillon, and I didn't even bother answering the door because I was so pissed at you for going off to Mom. That's on me."

I nodded, remembering that cold night that I had stood out on Aiden's porch, banging my hand on the door, willing him to come out so we could just talk. But Aiden had been so pissed off, and then I had been so livid that nothing had happened at all. We lost so many years.

"I won't let that happen. I'm not leaving. We're going to talk shit out."

"Good," Aiden said. "Because if we don't, I'm going to kick your fucking ass. Because you're my fucking brother. You don't get to leave like that. You don't just get to say things are too hard."

"Same goes for you," I said, this time growling just a little bit. "And I don't know what's going on with you, but if you need us, we're here."

"I'm fine. You're the one who seems to be in the doghouse, though," Aiden said quickly.

"That much is true," Brendon put in. "Go get your girl."

"I'm going to. Because I'm a fucking asshole, but I love her."

"Yes, use those words. It's very sweet. Very romantic." Aiden lifted his glass up in cheers, and I rolled my eyes.

"Fine. I'm going to be a little late for my shift then, most likely. I have to go get my girl."

Dillon hooted, and Aiden shook his head, but Brendon was the one to reach out and stop me.

I frowned. "What? I'm not on until later tonight."

Brendon sighed. "Oh, that's fine, and I can work behind the bar if you end up not showing up at all."

"Please don't do that," Beckham called from the back, and we all laughed.

Brendon scowled. "I'm just fine as a bartender."

"No, you're not," Beckham called again.

My brother just stared, the tick at the corner of his mouth in full force. "Anyway, if we ignore that asshole—"

"Not an asshole. Just a better bartender!"

"Shut up, Beckham!"

"You're not my boss."

"Yes, I am. We all are. Anyway," Brendon continued, "I know we just talked about the whole not being a stalker thing and going to her house, but you really don't want to go to her house."

"Why?" I asked.

"Yeah, why?" Dillon added.

Brendon shrugged. "Because she's not there."

I narrowed my eyes. "And you would know this why?"

"Because I was talking to Harmony about it, and it seems that she, along with Sienna and Violet, are off in Colorado Springs visiting Mace for the day. They're having a nice family meal even though the Knight parents are out of town."

"You were talking with Harmony?" Aiden asked.

"Off-subject."

"No," I said softly, "that might not be off topic at all." I sighed. "I guess I'm driving down to Colorado Springs."

"You're going to go grovel in front of her entire family?" Dillon asked. "That's actually pretty good. Groveling in front of others accentuates the groveling I think. It probably adds more points for later grovels, too. So, yes, do that."

I threw my hands up into the air. "Where are you finding these things? Is there a special book I should be reading about groveling and how to deal with women?" I asked, but I wasn't actually joking just then.

Aiden and Brendon laughed, but Dillon just grinned. "My ex-girlfriend really liked romance novels, so I started reading them with her. You learn a lot about women by reading romance. You should pick up a book. They're interesting, and there's some hot sex in there, so that's a plus. Don't worry, they use condoms, so I get extra safe sex lessons. Plus, whenever one of the heroes is an asshole, he still gets the girl because he grovels. And he actually means it. So, do it. Mean it. Get down on your knees if you have to, but just do it well."

I looked at my little brother in an all-new light and blinked. "Romance novels?"

"I have a few on my phone that I can send you links to after you beg for forgiveness. Because no matter what happens, you're going to end up having to apologize again later for something that you do. It's what we do. We're men."

"Aren't you eighteen?" Aiden asked.

Dillon smiled wide. "Yes, but I know all."

"Yeah, not so much," Brendon said but pulled out his phone anyway. "So, where should I start?"

As Aiden also had his phone out, I just laughed, then shook my head and walked out of the bar, knowing I had a place to be.

The drive wasn't going to be fun on my way to Colorado Springs to go see my girl, but I needed to grovel. If my little brother was on the right track, I needed to bow and scrape well.

CHAPTER NINETEEN

Love you. Always

  - Allison in a text to Violet

VIOLET

I WAS OKAY. I was better than okay. Mostly because I was out of my house with people that I loved, and I knew that with just a few more breaths, I would be fine.

I had called Mace the night before, and he had told me that he was going to come and get me and that I wasn't going to sleep alone in my house. That I was going to be just fine, and that I was going to find a therapist that worked for me, and we were going to get through this.

My big brother was a lot of things, and amazing was just one of them.

He was a little older than Sienna and me, so there'd always been some distance between us, but no matter what, he was there for us. And he was there for me today.

I ended up driving myself to Colorado Springs after letting Sienna know that I was going to spend the night at Mace's. I didn't have to work until Monday, so I planned to take some time for myself. I might even take Monday and Tuesday off, too, because I was allowed to when I had the vacation time. I might as well use it for my mental health.

I wasn't depressed, at least I didn't think so. I did not have thoughts of ending my life or doing anything to harm myself. But I needed to work out my feelings about Allison, and I needed to get through my grief. And to do that, I needed to talk to someone beyond my friends and family.

I was aware of that, and I was going to lean on my friends while I did it.

So now, I was at Mace's house, his fiancée leaning into him as their daughter Daisy danced around the kitchen.

Sienna and Harmony were with me in the living room, laughing as we ate some appetizers and waited for dinner. We were doing an early meal since it was the afternoon and Daisy wanted to play, but I didn't mind. I was surrounded by people I loved who loved me.

And, yes, we all needed to work through our emotions and our feelings, but we were doing it. And I wasn't afraid to ask for help. I'd always been a little bit scared to ask for help because I had to deal with my migraines and then the fact that I was worried about school and then my divorce and Cameron and all of that. It was hard for me to want to ask, knowing that I might ask too much.

But I was going to get over that, even if it annoyed me sometimes.

"Okay, so we have cheese. Lots of cheese." Adrienne grinned from the kitchen, and I looked over at her.

"What is it with you Montgomerys and cheese? It's like every time we come over here, it's cheese this and cheese that."

"One does not mock the cheese," Adrienne said serenely.

"Cheese, it's good!" Daisy exclaimed, and we all laughed.

"Seriously, though," Mace said quickly. "Don't mess with cheese with the Montgomerys. At least the Colorado Springs ones. Thea, Adrienne's sister? She's insane with the cheese."

"Hey, I'm going to tell her you said that. And then you're not going to get the brie with the pepper jelly on top. You know, the stuff made from the gods. It's like ambrosia."

"Okay, I retract my statement. I will never, ever mention anything bad about cheese."

My brother looked me directly in the eyes with a very somber expression. "Because that cheese is the best thing I've ever had in my life, and I will not risk it. Never. Not even for a joke."

"Mace got weird," Sienna said, not quite whispering in my ear.

"Very, very weird," I agreed.

"I don't know," Harmony said, shrugging. "I kind of agree with him about the cheese. I've had some of that pepper jelly. It's pretty amazing."

"No, you had pepper jelly," Mace said, "but you've never had *Thea's* pepper jelly." He kissed his fingertips like a chef. "The best thing in the world."

"And yet we're not going to have any tonight?" I asked, my stomach suddenly rumbling. "Because I feel the more we talk about it, the more we should actually have it."

"It's not like Beetlejuice where you say it three times, and it just shows up," Adrienne said dryly as she set a cheese platter down on the table. "But I have three types of cheeses for you. Only three because I get a little overwhelmed by more than that. Now, if we were at Thea's table, we'd have like seven. But that's just her and Dimitri, they're kind of special like that."

I shook my head, laughing, and put a piece of Havarti on a cracker. I really liked cheese, apparently not as much as some people, but to each their own.

"I love you, Auntie Violet," Daisy said softly, hugging me.

Daisy had hugged me more in the past twelve hours than I thought she had for the past month. Maybe she assumed I needed it, or perhaps she just needed it, too. I knew Daisy missed Allison, all of us did. And holding onto the little girl, the bit of my brother that was all the best parts rolled into one—daisies and unicorns and puppies—just told me that I had made the right decision in making sure that I was okay. All of us were hurting in little and different ways, and it was okay. It was okay to talk about it, it was okay to miss Allison. It was okay to be completely confused about why we were where we were.

We were just finishing up the cheese course and getting ready to head into the dining room for the rest of the meal when my phone buzzed.

"Is it Cameron?" Sienna asked quickly.

"Do I need to kick his ass?" Mace asked. "Because I wasn't allowed to do it before. I deserve an ass-kicking."

"Yes, you do deserve an ass-kicking." Adrienne grinned.

Mace scowled. "I meant I deserve to kick his ass. I misspoke. Shut up."

"Don't tell your fiancée to shut up," Sienna snapped. "Violet, is it Cameron?"

I looked down at my phone and groaned. "No, it's the end of the world."

"Is it Kent or is it Lynn?" Harmony asked.

"I never liked Uncle Kent," Daisy said. "He was a butthead."

"Daisy!" Adrienne said quickly. Of course, there were little red splotches on her cheekbones, so I had a feeling that Daisy had learned that phrase about Kent from someone in the family, and it wasn't me.

I just shook my head. "Oh, he is a butthead. But I'm

going to answer this. Who knows, maybe Lynn is hurt or something and can't come into work."

I waved off their looks, knowing that I probably shouldn't answer, but I wasn't a mean person, and my goal in life at least for now was to face my demons, even if one of them was named Kent.

I figured the call was about to drop soon since it took so long for me to answer. When I did, Kent's very chiseled and boring face came on the screen, his eyes narrowed.

"Hi, Kent. How can I help you?"

"I thought you weren't going to answer." He paused. I saw him frown, and I wondered what the hell this could be about. "But I'm glad you did."

"Good. How can I help?"

"Lynn and I just wanted to ask you something. No, we wanted to say something."

"Okay." I had a really bad feeling about this, but it wasn't like I could hang up. And, frankly, Kent hadn't called me since the divorce was final, so I was kind of wondering what exactly he had to say. It wasn't like Lynn had been the one to call me. And we worked together. It would make sense if she called me. Maybe not on a Sunday, but you never know.

"Well," Kent cleared his throat. The phone rustled, and then it moved to landscape mode, so both he and Lynn were in the frame.

Great. This was going to help me. Totally.

"We just wanted to let you know that we're expecting. A baby. We're having a baby."

I waited for the shock, waited for it to hurt. I was expecting the pain that had come when I saw Cameron standing there with a woman next to him. I was waiting for that infinitesimal amount of time to pass where I thought that my trust in Cameron wasn't good enough.

That never came.

And honestly, I didn't think it would come at all.

"And?"

Kent cleared his throat, and Lynn gave me that sickly sweet little smile of hers. The one that said she pitied me.

I really hated her. Not because she used to be my friend and was now married to my ex-husband. Not because of the cheating. Because of those looks.

"Well, we know it's been really hard at work with how things are."

I held up my hand and realized that they couldn't actually see that, so I just shook my head. "No, you're going to stop right there. Live your life. Love your life. I'm doing the best to live mine. I've learned the hard way that others can't always live their lives."

They gave me a strange look, and I swallowed back some tears. Not because of them, but because of those who I had lost because they couldn't live the life they wanted. Or some other reason that I just didn't know.

"I'm happy for you. Happy that you're moving on. But it's not my business. It never was." And so I hung up and really hoped that they wouldn't call again. Because, frankly, I wasn't in the mood to keep hitting ignore.

My ex-husband and his wife were having a baby. That was great. Seriously great for them. Kent had always wanted kids, and while I wanted some in the future, the two of us having kids had never really been a big part of my plan. Yes, that was probably on me. I hadn't really felt when I was with him. But I did feel when I was with Cameron. And so, the next time Cameron called, I was going to answer. I wasn't going to be so far into my head that I would run away again.

I was just walking back to the dining room when the doorbell rang. I frowned.

"Can you get that, Violet?" Mace asked from the kitchen. "My hands are full, and you're closer."

"Sure. But you're lazy," I called out and then laughed when I knew my brother was trying to flip me off from beneath the pot holder.

I opened the door and then froze.

"Cameron."

"You're here. Oh, thank God. I had Brendon text me the address, though I don't know exactly how he got it, and I'm not going to ask. But I was really afraid that I read it wrong and would end up at the wrong door. But you're here."

I swallowed hard and looked at him. "Yeah, I'm here. And you're here."

"I'm here to say I'm sorry."

I shook my head and then moved forward to put my hands on his chest. Damn, I missed him. "No, you don't have to be sorry. That was so not on you. I think I just got overwhelmed and I walked away, and then I couldn't answer my phone. Couldn't because it was too much, not because I didn't want to. And I'm sorry."

He blinked. "Really? Wait, no, I'm supposed to be the one groveling here. I'm the one who let that woman touch me."

I shook my head and bit my lip. "Let's never talk about that again because that was so not on you. I'm the one who walked away because I got overwhelmed. I did exactly what you did. We really suck at communicating." I said quickly. "I'm so sorry."

"No, that's my line. Seriously. I'm the one who sucks at communicating. I'm sorry." He was almost growling the words now, and I had a feeling that he had practiced a whole speech and I was ruining it for him.

"I love you." His eyes widened, and I continued. "I love you so damn much. I loved you when you left, and I loved you even more when you came back. I just didn't realize it. There are a lot of things that we need to talk about, but first...first you need to know something. I love you and I'm sorry for walking away like I did. I'm sorry for it being too much and me not knowing how to handle it. I did exactly what you did, and now that I'm thinking about it in retrospect, I'm really ashamed."

Cameron shook his head and cupped my face, kissing me hard. "I came here to apologize to you. To grovel as

Dillon said. He said a good grovel is exactly what was needed."

"He told me he was reading those romance books and learning about women." I laughed when Cameron rolled his eyes. "No, really. He mentioned it. I guess that's where he learned the word."

"That's what he tells me. But I love you so fucking much, Violet. We need to do this better. We need to be better at this. We're older now, we have more experience. We can't be stupid at this."

I kissed him then and fell into him. "I love you so much."

"And I love you so fucking much." I sighed at his words, let them sink into me. "I've loved you for so long, and I made so many bad decisions that broke everything that I had with the people I loved. With people who loved me. And I'm never going to do that again. Yes, I'm going to make mistakes, but I'm never going to make this mistake again. So, anytime there's an issue where it gets to be too much, we need to talk it out. Or we need a sign or something to say that we need some space. Something so we don't end up in this situation again. Because, Violet? I can't live my life the way that I know I need to if you're not in it. I need you by my side. I need you." He let out a breath. "You're the one who talked about breaking before, but I know I'd be broken without you, I was already breaking without you before. So, let's do this thing. Let's figure this out together. Because I love you so much."

"I don't want to ever break again. Not like that. And I do

trust you. I'm the one that walked away this time. But I'm not going to do it again. So, come on inside, Cameron. Let's have dinner with the Knights, let's take it one step at a time. Because I love you. And I want you in my life just like you said. And we'll come up with that sign when things get to be too much. We'll come up with everything."

And so, I took his hand and led him into the living room.

I knew we had more to talk about, that there would be more emotions and feelings that we needed to deal with as time passed. I knew I wasn't completely over losing Allison, and I never would be.

But that was just one part of my life, a part that I would get through by talking with good friends, with family, and with my man by my side.

The man I loved with all of my heart.

We'd ended up apart for too long because of mistakes we couldn't erase, but now we were together in spite of those. And that meant more than anything.

That was a promise.

A promise worth keeping.

EPILOGUE

CAMERON

THE BEER WAS POURING, the tapas were popping, and people were laughing, spending money, and having a good time. The fact that we were on week eight of the pool tournament, and I was in second place along with my girl meant that we were doing pretty damn well for ourselves.

The bar was doing great, and I knew we would be just fine, no matter what happened next. The Connolly brothers and Jack's place, The Connolly Brewery, were going to thrive.

And as I wrapped my arms around my woman, kissing her hard before she bent over so she could take her shot, I knew that my girl and I would be just fine. Plus, as I took a few steps back to watch her ass as she moved, I knew I was a very, very lucky man.

"You know, you're making it very hard for me to concentrate when you keep looking at me like that," Violet said, shaking her hips.

I just grinned, keeping my eyes on her ass. "Well, I can't help it. I kind of like it."

She looked over her shoulder and mock glared. "Kind of like it? I don't think so. You're supposed to love it."

"If you two could stop discussing Violet's ass and everything you'd like to do with it and get to actually playing pool, that would be wonderful," Brendon said, chalking up his cue. He met Harmony's gaze, and both of them started laughing at a joke I probably wasn't privy to. Didn't really understand what was so funny about the fact that I liked watching Violet's ass, but...whatever.

There was shouting from the kitchen, and I winced. "Damn it," Brendon muttered under his breath. "You want me to go handle that?"

"I've got it," Dillon said quickly before running back there. The fact that the shouting was between Aiden and Sienna was not lost on anyone. They had been disqualified the previous week at another bar because they had been fighting and hadn't actually finished the game. So, they weren't even in the tournament tonight. I didn't know why they were fighting, but I figured we'd learn eventually. We were all too close these days for us not to figure it out. Dillon was a brave soul for going back to the kitchen. But Sienna liked him, and Aiden and Dillon had created a bond over the past couple of months and seemed to understand each other better than they had before.

Things were looking good, and I was damn happy.

Violet missed her shot, cursed under her breath, and Brendon and Harmony smiled at each other before Brendon went for his own shot.

"Sorry about that," Violet said.

"No worries, this is just fun at this point. The next tournament is getting set, we have another special going on, people are crowding the bar. I'm happy." I kissed her temple, and she leaned into me, so I wrapped my arms around her.

Things hadn't been easy for the past two months, and I knew they wouldn't be completely easy going forward either. But that was fine. All three of the girls had started going to therapy, and I had even gone with Violet a couple of times. I'd had a therapist when I was younger, but then I quit going, but I actually liked going and talking with Violet's so I might end up getting one of my own. That was if I didn't just keep talking with Beckham or my brothers behind the bar. They said a bartender was like a therapist sometimes, and most of the time, Beckham usually ended up feeling like he was qualified for both jobs—or so he said.

Therapy or not, I loved the woman in my arms, and one day I would ask her to marry me. Not yet, not when everything was just a little too fresh, a little too raw. I wanted to make sure that she was settled and ready for what we faced.

She had grant money coming in for work, and Lynn was

no longer working at the school because she was pregnant and didn't want to be near some of the chemicals and had decided to be a stay-at-home mom. That meant that Violet didn't have to deal with her ex-husband or anything having to do with him, and she could actually do what she loved and focus on it.

I knew she was still dealing with grief over Allison. That would likely be never-ending even as it changed.

But we had each other, and we trusted each other.

And maybe Dillon was right, and reading romance novels had helped just a little. It felt like I could get into Violet's head just by reading someone else's words regarding what a woman might actually want. Of course, it was fun reading it to each other, and especially when we got to the dirty bits and could try and act out some of the scenes to see if it was physically possible. It was research, after all.

Brendon missed his shot, so I went for mine. I made two balls and then missed the third.

I cursed at myself, but Harmony looked like she was on cloud nine. She sauntered over to the table, pulled her hair back from her face, and sank their last two balls and then the eight ball in quick succession.

I felt like we had been hustled, even though I'd been watching her get better over the last two months.

"That's my girl," Brendon called out, spinning Harmony around. She pushed at his shoulder, and the two of them separated, not looking at each other but still smiling.

I rolled my eyes at them as they started doing an actual synchronized dance that I had no idea when they'd had the time to practice, but apparently, they were competitive when it came to pool.

Violet pouted for a second before laughing at the spectacle that was the dance before turning around in my arms and kissing me on the chin.

"Well, we got second place. We still get money, right?"

"Yeah, a few bucks. Kind of pissed off that Mr. Moneybags over there got most of it, but whatever."

Violet kissed my chin again. "How about I use some of my winnings to buy you a beer."

"So you can give more money back to the bar? I think I like this."

"Sounds like a plan to me. Because I plan on hanging out with you here for a long time to come, Cameron Connolly. So, you better keep that sign above the door and the Connollys within these walls. Because I love it here. And I love you."

"I love you, too, Violet Knight." And I kissed her, ignoring the catcalls from around us. People were coming in to congratulate the other team and then taking the pool table for their own, enjoying the time, having fun, drinking and just being.

But I only had eyes for the woman in my arms. I knew that everything was going to be all right, just like she'd said. Because I had Violet. I had my family. I had this bar.

And I didn't need to keep running away from things. Finally.

Next in the Fractured Connections Series:

Harmony and Brendon in Shouldn't Have You.

A NOTE FROM CARRIE ANN RYAN

Thank you so much for reading **BREAKING WITHOUT YOU.** I do hope if you liked this story, that you would please leave a review! Reviews help authors *and* readers.

This story wasn't easy to write. But it was one that I needed to get on paper. This series is heavy, I know that, but in the end, there is hope, there is that happily ever after. I wanted to write a series where there is love even when it doesn't feel like there can be.

I'm honored you're reading this series and I do hope you continue on. This is possibly one of my most personal series and I'm blessed in the fact I get to write it.

Next up is Harmony and Brendon, and if you know my personal story, you know this book will be hard, but then again, there is a reason we all love reading HEAs.

After that, Sienna and Aiden have some explaining to

do. And Meadow and Beckham surprised me and screamed that they needed their stories as well.

BTW, in case you didn't know, Mace and Adrienne had their story in Fallen Ink as the Fractured Series is part of the Montgomery Ink world!

And if you're new to my books, you can start anywhere within the my interconnected series and catch up! Each book is a stand alone, so jump around!

Don't miss out on the Montgomery Ink World!

- Montgomery Ink (The Denver Montgomerys)
- Montgomery Ink: Colorado Springs (The Colorado Springs Montgomery Cousins)
- Montgomery Ink: Boulder (The Boulder Montgomery Cousins)
- Gallagher Brothers (Jake's Brothers from Ink Enduring)
- Whiskey and Lies (Tabby's Brothers from Ink Exposed)
- Fractured Connections (Mace's sisters from Fallen Ink)
- Less Than (Dimitri's siblings from Restless Ink)

If you want to make sure you know what's coming next from me, you can sign up for my newsletter at www.CarrieAnnRyan.com; follow me on twitter at @CarrieAnnRyan, or like my Facebook page. I also have a Facebook Fan Club where we have trivia, chats, and other goodies. You guys are the reason I get to do what I do and I thank you.

Make sure you're signed up for my MAILING LIST so you can know when the next releases are available as well as find giveaways and FREE READS.

Happy Reading!

The Fractured Connections Series:
A Montgomery Ink Spin Off Series
Book 1: Breaking Without You
Book 2: Shouldn't Have You
Book 3: Falling With You
Book 4: Taken With You

Want to keep up to date with the next Carrie Ann Ryan Release? Receive Text Alerts easily!

Text CARRIE to 24587

ABOUT CARRIE ANN RYAN

Carrie Ann Ryan is the New York Times and USA Today bestselling author of contemporary and paranormal romance. Her works include the Montgomery Ink, Redwood Pack, Talon Pack, and Gallagher Brothers series, which have sold over 2.0 million books worldwide. She started writing while in graduate school for her advanced degree in chemistry and hasn't stopped since. Carrie Ann has written over fifty novels and novellas with more in the works. When she's not writing about bearded tattooed men or alpha wolves that need to find their mates, she's reading as much as she can and exploring the world of baking and gourmet cooking.

www.CarrieAnnRyan.com

MORE FROM CARRIE ANN RYAN

Montgomery Ink: Colorado Springs
Book 1: Fallen Ink
Book 2: Restless Ink
Book 2.5: Ashes to Ink
Book 3: Jagged Ink
Book 3.5: Ink by Numbers

The Fractured Connections Series:
A Montgomery Ink Spin Off Series
Book 1: Breaking Without You
Book 2: Shouldn't Have You
Book 3: Falling With You
Book 4: Taken With You

The Montgomery Ink: Boulder Series:
Book 1: Wrapped in Ink

Book 2: Sated in Ink

The Less Than Series:
A Montgomery Ink Spin Off Series
Book 1: Breathless With Her
Book 2: Reckless With You
Book 3: Shameless With Him

The Elements of Five Series:
Book 1: From Breath and Ruin
Book 2: From Flame and Ash

Montgomery Ink:
Book 0.5: Ink Inspired
Book 0.6: Ink Reunited
Book 1: Delicate Ink
Book 1.5: Forever Ink
Book 2: Tempting Boundaries
Book 3: Harder than Words
Book 4: Written in Ink
Book 4.5: Hidden Ink
Book 5: Ink Enduring
Book 6: Ink Exposed
Book 6.5: Adoring Ink
Book 6.6: Love, Honor, & Ink
Book 7: Inked Expressions
Book 7.3: Dropout
Book 7.5: Executive Ink

Book 8: Inked Memories
Book 8.5: Inked Nights
Book 8.7: Second Chance Ink

The Gallagher Brothers Series:
A Montgomery Ink Spin Off Series

Book 1: Love Restored
Book 2: Passion Restored
Book 3: Hope Restored

The Whiskey and Lies Series:
A Montgomery Ink Spin Off Series

Book 1: Whiskey Secrets
Book 2: Whiskey Reveals
Book 3: Whiskey Undone

The Talon Pack:

Book 1: Tattered Loyalties
Book 2: An Alpha's Choice
Book 3: Mated in Mist
Book 4: Wolf Betrayed
Book 5: Fractured Silence
Book 6: Destiny Disgraced
Book 7: Eternal Mourning
Book 8: Strength Enduring
Book 9: Forever Broken

Redwood Pack Series:

Book 1: An Alpha's Path

Book 2: A Taste for a Mate

Book 3: Trinity Bound

Redwood Pack Box Set (Contains Books 1-3)

Book 3.5: A Night Away

Book 4: Enforcer's Redemption

Book 4.5: Blurred Expectations

Book 4.7: Forgiveness

Book 5: Shattered Emotions

Book 6: Hidden Destiny

Book 6.5: A Beta's Haven

Book 7: Fighting Fate

Book 7.5: Loving the Omega

Book 7.7: The Hunted Heart

Book 8: Wicked Wolf

The Complete Redwood Pack Box Set (Contains Books 1-7.7)

The Branded Pack Series:
(Written with Alexandra Ivy)

Book 1: Stolen and Forgiven

Book 2: Abandoned and Unseen

Book 3: Buried and Shadowed

Dante's Circle Series:

Book 1: Dust of My Wings

Book 2: Her Warriors' Three Wishes

Book 3: An Unlucky Moon

The Dante's Circle Box Set (Contains Books 1-3)

Book 3.5: His Choice

Book 4: Tangled Innocence

Book 5: Fierce Enchantment

Book 6: An Immortal's Song

Book 7: Prowled Darkness

The Complete Dante's Circle Series (Contains Books 1-7)

Holiday, Montana Series:

Book 1: Charmed Spirits

Book 2: Santa's Executive

Book 3: Finding Abigail

The Holiday, Montana Box Set (Contains Books 1-3)

Book 4: Her Lucky Love

Book 5: Dreams of Ivory

The Complete Holiday, Montana Box Set (Contains Books 1-5)

The Happy Ever After Series:

Flame and Ink

Ink Ever After

Single Title:

Finally Found You

EXCERPT: WHISKEY SECRETS

From New York Times Bestselling Author Carrie Ann Ryan's Whiskey and Lies

Whiskey Secrets

Shocking pain slammed into his skull and down his back. Dare Collins did his best not to scream in the middle of his own bar. He slowly stood up and rubbed the back of his head since he'd been distracted and hit it on the countertop. Since the thing was made of solid wood and thick as hell, he was surprised he hadn't given himself a concussion. But since he didn't see double, he had a feeling once his long night was over, he'd just have to make the throbbing go away with a glass of Macallan.

There was nothing better than a glass of smooth whiskey or an ice-cold mug of beer after a particularly long day.

Which one Dare chose each night depended on not only his mood but also those around him. So was the life of a former cop turned bartender.

He had a feeling he'd be going for the whiskey and not a woman tonight—like most nights if he were honest. It had been a long day of inventory and no-show staff members. Meaning he had a headache from hell, and it looked as if he'd be working open to close when he truly didn't want to. But that's what happened when one was the owner of a bar and restaurant rather than just a manager or bartender—like he was with the Old Whiskey Restaurant and Bar.

It didn't help that his family had been in and out of the place all day for one reason or another—his brothers and parents either wanting something to eat or having a question that needed to be answered right away where a phone call or text wouldn't suffice. His mom and dad had mentioned more than once that he needed to be ready for their morning meeting, and he had a bad feeling in his gut about what that would mean for him later. But he pushed that from his thoughts because he was used to things in his life changing on a dime. He'd left the force for a reason, after all.

Enough of that.

He loved his family, he really did, but sometimes, they—his parents in particular—gave him a headache.

Since his mom and dad still ran the Old Whiskey Inn above his bar, they were constantly around, working their tails off at odd jobs that were far too hard for them at their ages, but they were all just trying to earn a living. When they weren't handling business for the inn, they were fixing problems upstairs that Dare wished they'd let him help with.

While he'd have preferred to call it a night and head back to his place a few blocks away, he knew that wouldn't happen tonight. Since his bartender, Rick, had called in sick at the last minute—as well as two of Dare's waitresses from the bar—Dare was pretty much screwed.

And if he wallowed just a little bit more, he might hear a tiny violin playing in his ear. He needed to get a grip and get over it. Working late and dealing with other people's mistakes was part of his job description, and he was usually fine with that.

Apparently, he was just a little off tonight. And since he knew himself well, he had a feeling it was because he was nearing the end of his time without his kid. Whenever he spent too many days away from Nathan, he acted like a crabby asshole. Thankfully, his weekend was coming up.

"Solving a hard math problem over there, or just daydreaming? Because that expression on your face looks like you're working your brain too hard. I'm surprised I don't see smoke coming out of your ears." Fox asked as he walked up to the bar, bringing Dare out of his thoughts. Dare had been pulling drafts and cleaning glasses mindlessly while in his head, but he was glad for the distraction, even if it annoyed him that he needed one.

Dare shook his head and flipped off his brother. "Suck me."

The bar was busy that night, so Fox sat down on one of the empty stools and grinned. "Nice way to greet your customers." He glanced over his shoulder before looking back at Dare and frowning. "Where are Rick and the rest of your staff?"

Dare barely held back a growl. "Out sick. Either there's really a twenty-four-hour stomach bug going around and I'm going to be screwed for the next couple of days, or they're all out on benders."

Fox cursed under his breath before hopping off his stool and going around the side of the large oak and maple bar to help out. That was Dare's family in a nutshell—they dropped everything whenever one of them needed help, and nobody even had to ask for it. Since Dare sucked at asking for help on a good day, he was glad that Fox knew what he needed without him having to say it.

Without asking, Fox pulled up a few drink orders and began mixing them with the skill of a long-time barkeep. Since Fox owned the small town newspaper—the Whiskey Chronicle—Dare was still surprised sometimes at how deft his younger brother was at working alongside him. Of course, even his parents, his older brother Loch, and his younger sister Tabby knew their way around the bar.

Just not as well as Dare did. Considering that this was *his* job, he was grateful for that.

He loved his family, his bar, and hell, he even loved his little town on the outskirts of Philly. Whiskey, Pennsylvania was like most other small towns in his state where some parts were new additions, and others were old stone buildings from the Revolutionary or Civil war eras with add-ons —like his.

And with a place called Whiskey, everyone attached the label where they could. Hence the town paper, his bar, and most of the other businesses around town. Only Loch's business really stood out with Loch's Security and Gym down the street, but that was just like Loch to be a little different yet still part of the town.

Whiskey had been named as such because of its old bootlegging days. It used to be called something else, but since Prohibition, the town had changed its name and cashed in on it. Whiskey was one of the last places in the country to keep Prohibition on the books, even with the nationwide decree. They'd fought to keep booze illegal, not for puritan reasons, but because their bootlegging market had helped the township thrive. Dare knew there was a lot more to it than that, but those were the stories the leaders told the tourists, and it helped with the flare.

Whiskey was located right on the Delaware River, so it overlooked New Jersey but was still on the Pennsylvania side of things. The main bridge that connected the two states through Whiskey and Ridge on the New Jersey side was one of the tourist spots for people to drive over and walk so they could be in two states at once while over the Delaware River.

Their town was steeped in history, and close enough to where George Washington had crossed the Delaware that they were able to gain revenue on the reenactments for the tourists, thus helping keep their town afloat.

The one main road through Whiskey that not only housed Loch's and Dare's businesses but also many of the other shops and restaurants in the area, was always jammed with cars and people looking for places to parallel park. Dare's personal parking lot for the bar and inn was a hot commodity.

And while he might like time to himself some days, he knew he wouldn't trade Whiskey's feel for any other place. They were a weird little town that was a mesh of history and newcomers, and he wouldn't trade it for the world. His sister Tabby might have moved out west and found her love and her place with the Montgomerys in Denver, but Dare knew he'd only ever find his home here.

Sure, he'd had a few flings in Denver when he visited his sister, but he knew they'd never be more than one night or two. Hell, he was the king of flings these days, and that was for good reason. He didn't need commitment or attachments beyond his family and his son, Nathan.

Time with Nathan's mom had proven that to him, after all.

"You're still daydreaming over there," Fox called out from the other side of the bar. "You okay?"

Dare nodded, frowning. "Yeah, I think I need more caffeine or something since my mind keeps wandering." He pasted on his trademark grin and went to help one of the new arrivals who'd taken a seat at the bar. Dare wasn't the broody one of the family—that honor went to Loch—and he hated when he acted like it.

"What can I get you?" he asked a young couple that had taken two empty seats at the bar. They had matching wedding bands on their fingers but looked to be in their early twenties.

He couldn't imagine being married that young. Hell, he'd never been married, and he was in his mid-thirties now. He hadn't married Monica even though she'd given him Nathan, and even now, he wasn't sure they'd have ever taken that step even if they had stayed together. She had Auggie now, and he had...well, he had his bar.

That wasn't depressing at all.

"Two Yuenglings please, draft if you have it," the guy said, smiling.

Dare nodded. "Gonna need to see your IDs, but I do have it on tap for you." As Yuengling was a Pennsylvania beer, not having it outside the bottle would be stupid even in a town that prided itself on whiskey.

The couple pulled out their IDs, and Dare checked them quickly. Since both were now the ripe age of twenty-two, he went to pull them their beers and set out their check since they weren't looking to run a tab.

Another woman with long, caramel brown hair with hints of red came to sit at the edge of the bar. Her hair lay in loose waves down her back and she had on a sexy-as-fuck green dress that draped over her body to showcase sexy curves and legs that seemed to go on forever. The garment didn't have sleeves so he could see the toned muscles in her arms work as she picked up a menu to look at it. When she looked up, she gave him a dismissive glance before focusing on the menu again. He held back a sigh. Not in the mood to deal with whatever that was about, he let Fox take care of her and put her from his mind. No use dealing with a woman who clearly didn't want him near, even if it were just to take a drink order. Funny, he usually had to speak to a female before making her want him out of the picture. At least, that's what he'd learned from Monica.

And why the hell was he thinking about his ex again? He usually only thought of her in passing when he was talking to Nathan or hanging out with his kid for the one weekend a month the custody agreement let Dare have him. Having been in a dangerous job and then becoming a bartender didn't look good to some lawyers it seemed, at least when Monica had fought for full custody after Nathan was born.

He pushed those thoughts from his mind, however, not in the mood to scare anyone with a scowl on his face by remembering how his ex had looked down on him for his occupation even though she'd been happy to slum it with him when it came to getting her rocks off.

Dare went through the motions of mixing a few more drinks before leaving Fox to tend to the bar so he could go check on the restaurant part of the building.

Since the place had originally been an old stone inn on both floors instead of just the top one, it was set up a little differently than most newer buildings around town. The bar was off to one side; the restaurant area where they served delicious, higher-end entrees and tapas was on the other. Most people needed a reservation to sit down and eat in the main restaurant area, but the bar also had seating for dinner, only their menu wasn't quite as extensive and ran closer to bar food.

In the past, he'd never imagined he would be running something like this, even though his parents had run a smaller version of it when he was a kid. But none of his siblings had been interested in taking over once his parents wanted to retire from the bar part and only run the inn. When Dare decided to leave the force only a few years in, he'd found his place here, however reluctantly.

Being a cop hadn't been for him, just like being in a relationship. He'd thought he would be able to do the former, but life had taken a turn, and he'd faced his mortality far sooner than he bargained for. Apparently, being a gruff, perpetually single bar owner was more his speed, and he was pretty damn good at it, too. Most days, anyway.

His house manager over on the restaurant side was running from one thing to another, but from the outside, no one would have noticed. Claire was just that good. She was in her early fifties and already a grandmother, but she didn't look a day over thirty-five with her smooth, dark skin and bright smile. Good genes and makeup did wonders— according to her anyway. He'd be damned if he'd say that.

His mother and Tabby had taught him *something* over the years.

The restaurant was short-staffed but managing, and he was grateful he had Claire working long hours like he did. He oversaw it all, but he knew he couldn't have done it without her. After making sure she didn't need anything, he headed back to the bar to relieve Fox. The rush was finally dying down now, and his brother could just sit back and enjoy a beer since Dare knew he'd already worked a long day at the paper.

By the time the restaurant closed and the bar only held a few dwindling costumers, Dare was ready to go to bed and forget the whole lagging day. Of course, he still had to close out the two businesses and talk to both Fox and Loch since his older brother had shown up a few moments ago. Maybe he'd get them to help him close out so he wouldn't be here until midnight. He must be tired if the thought of closing out was too much for him.

"So, Rick didn't show, huh?" Loch asked as he stood up from his stool. His older brother started cleaning up beside Fox, and Dare held back a smile. He'd have to repay them in something other than beer, but he knew they were working alongside him because they were family and had the time; they weren't doing it for rewards.

"Nope. Shelly and Kayla didn't show up either." Dare resisted the urge to grind his teeth at that. "Thanks for helping. I'm exhausted and wasn't in the mood to deal with this all alone."

"That's what we're here for," Loch said with a shrug.

"By the way, you have any idea what this seven a.m. meeting tomorrow is about?" Fox asked after a moment. "They're putting Tabby on speaker phone for it and everything."

Dare let out a sigh. "I'm not in the mood to deal with any meeting that early. I have no idea what it's going to be about, but I have a bad feeling."

"Seems like they have an announcement." Loch sat back down on his stool and scrolled through his phone. He was constantly working or checking on his daughter, so his phone was strapped to him at all times. Misty had to be with Loch's best friend, Ainsley, since his brother worked that night. Ainsley helped out when Loch needed a night to work or see Dare. Loch had full custody of Misty, and being a single father wasn't easy.

Dare had a feeling no matter what his parents had to say, things were going to be rocky after the morning meeting. His parents were caring, helpful, and always wanted the best for their family. That also meant they tended to be slightly over-bearing in the most loving way possible.

"Well, shit."

It looked like he'd go without whiskey *or* a woman tonight.

Of course, an image of the woman with gorgeous hair and that look of disdain filled his mind, and he held back a sigh. Once again, Dare was a glutton for punishment, even in his thoughts.

The next morning, he cupped his mug of coffee in his hands and prayed his eyes would stay open. He'd stupidly gotten caught up on paperwork the night before and was now running on about three hours of sleep.

Loch sat in one of the booths with Misty, watching as she colored in her coloring book. She was the same age as Nathan, which Dare always appreciated since the cousins could grow up like siblings—on weekends when Dare had Nathan that was. The two kids got along great, and he hoped that continued throughout the cootie phases kids seemed to get sporadically.

Fox sat next to Dare at one of the tables with his laptop open. Since his brother owned the town paper, he was always up-to-date on current events and was even now typing up something.

They had Dare's phone between them with Tabby on the other line, though she wasn't saying anything. Her fiancé, Alex, was probably near as well since those two seemed to be attached at the hip. Considering his future brother-in-law adored Tabby, Dare didn't mind that as much as he probably should have as a big brother.

The elder Collinses stood at the bar, smiles on their faces, yet Dare saw nervousness in their stances. He'd been a cop too long to miss it. They were up to something, and he had a feeling he wasn't going to like it.

"Just get it over with," Dare said, keeping his language

decent—not only for Misty but also because his mother would still take him by the ear if he cursed in front of her.

But because his tone had bordered on rude, his mother still raised a brow, and he sighed. Yep, he had a really bad feeling about this.

"Good morning to you, too, Dare," Bob Collins said with a snort and shook his head. "Well, since you're all here, even our baby girl, Tabby—"

"Not a baby, Dad!" Tabby called out from the phone, and the rest of them laughed, breaking the tension slightly.

"Yeah, we're not babies," Misty put in, causing everyone to laugh even harder.

"Anyway," Barbara Collins said with a twinkle in her eye. "We have an announcement to make." She rolled her shoulders back, and Dare narrowed his eyes. "As you know, your father and I have been nearing the age of retirement for a while now, but we still wanted to run our inn as innkeepers rather that merely owners."

"Finally taking a vacation?" Dare asked. His parents worked far too hard and wouldn't let their kids help them. He'd done what he could by buying the bar from them when he retired from the force and then built the restaurant himself.

"If you'd let me finish, young man, I'd let you know," his mother said coolly, though there was still warmth in her eyes. That was his mother in a nutshell. She'd reprimand, but soothe the sting, too.

"Sorry," he mumbled, and Fox coughed to cover up a

laugh. If Dare looked behind him, he figured he'd see Loch hiding a smile of his own.

Tabby laughed outright.

Damn little sisters.

"So, as I was saying, we've worked hard. But, lately, it seems like we've worked *too* hard." She looked over at his dad and smiled softly, taking her husband's hand. "It's time to make some changes around here."

Dare sat up straighter.

"We're retiring. Somewhat. The inn hasn't been doing as well as it did back when it was with your grandparents, and part of that is on the economy. But part of that is on us. What we want to do is renovate more and update the existing rooms and service. In order to do that and step back as innkeepers, we've hired a new person."

"You're kidding me, right?" Dare asked, frowning. "You can't just hire someone to take over and work in our building without even talking to us. And it's not like I have time to help her run it when she doesn't know how you like things."

"You won't be running it," Bob said calmly. "Not yet, anyway. Your mom and I haven't fully retired, and you know it. We've been running the inn for years, but now we want to step away. Something *you've* told us we should do. So, we hired someone. One who knows how to handle this kind of transition and will work with the construction crew and us. She has a lot of experience from working in Philly and New York and will be an asset."

Dare fisted his hands by his sides and blew out a breath.

They had to be fucking kidding. "It sounds like you've done your research and already made your decision. Without asking us. Without asking *me*."

His mother gave him a sad look. "We've always wanted to do this, Dare, you know that."

"Yes. But you should have talked to us. And renovating like this? I didn't know you wanted to. We could have helped." He didn't know why he was so angry, but being kept out of the loop was probably most of it.

His father signed. "We've been looking into this for years, even before you came back to Whiskey and bought the bar from us. And while it may seem like this is out of the blue, we've been doing the research for a while. Yes, we should have told you, but everything came up all at once recently, and we wanted to show you the plans when we had details rather than get your hopes up and end up not doing it."

Dare just blinked. There was so much in that statement —in *all* of those statements—that he couldn't quite process it. And though he could have yelled about any of it just then, his mind fixed on the one thing that annoyed him the most.

"So, you're going to have some city girl come into *my* place and order me around? I don't think so."

"And why not? Have a problem with listening to women?"

Dare stiffened because that last part hadn't come from his family. No. He turned toward the voice. It had come from the woman he'd seen the night before in the green dress.

And because fate liked to fuck with him, he had a feeling he knew *exactly* who this person was.

Their newly hired innkeeper.

And new thorn in his side.

Find out more in Whiskey Secrets.
To make sure you're up to date on all of Carrie Ann's releases, sign up for her mailing list HERE.

FALLEN INK

From New York Times Bestselling Author Carrie Ann Ryan's Whiskey and Lies

Fallen Ink

The Montgomery Ink series continues with a spin-off in Colorado Springs, where a familiar Montgomery finds her place in a new tattoo shop, and in the arms of her best friend.

Adrienne Montgomery is finally living her dreams. She's opened a tattoo shop with her brother, Shep, and two of her cousins from Denver and she's ready to take the city by storm with her art—as long as she can handle the pressure. When her new neighbors decide her shop isn't a great fit for the community, however, she'll have to lean on the one person she didn't expect to fall for along the way...her best friend.

Mace Knight takes pride in two things: his art and his daughter. He knows he's taking a risk by starting over in a new shop with the Montgomerys, but the stakes are even higher when he finds himself wanting Adrienne more than he thought possible.

The two fall fast and hard but they know the rules; they can't risk their friendship, no matter how hot it is between the sheets and how many people try to stand in their way.

Find out more in Fallen Ink.
To make sure you're up to date on all of Carrie Ann's releases, sign up for her mailing list HERE.

LOVE RESTORED

From New York Times Bestselling Author Carrie Ann Ryan's Gallagher Brothers series

Love Restored

In the first of a Montgomery Ink spin-off series from NYT Bestselling Author Carrie Ann Ryan, a broken man uncovers the truth of what it means to take a second chance with the most unexpected woman...

Graham Gallagher has seen it all. And when tragedy struck, lost it all. He's been the backbone of his brothers, the one they all rely on in their lives and business. And when it comes to falling in love and creating a life, he knows what it's like to have it all and watch it crumble. He's done with looking for another person to warm his bed, but apparently he didn't learn his lesson because the new piercer at Montgomery Ink tempts him like no other.

Blake Brennen may have been born a trust fund baby, but she's created a whole new life for herself in the world of ink, piercings, and freedom. Only the ties she'd thought she'd cut long ago aren't as severed as she'd believed. When she finds Graham constantly in her path, she knows from first glance that he's the wrong kind of guy for her. Except that Blake excels at making the wrong choice and Graham might be the ultimate temptation for the bad girl she'd thought long buried.

Find out more in Love Restored

To make sure you're up to date on all of Carrie Ann's releases, sign up for her mailing list HERE.

DELICATE INK

**From New York Times Bestselling Author Carrie
Ann Ryan's Montgomery Ink Series**

DELICATE INK

On the wrong side of thirty, Austin Montgomery is ready to
settle down. Unfortunately, his inked sleeves and scruffy
beard isn't the suave business appearance some women
crave. Only finding a woman who can deal with his job, as a
tattoo artist and owner of Montgomery Ink, his seven
meddling siblings, and his own gruff attitude won't be easy.

Finding a man is the last thing on Sierra Elder's mind. A
recent transplant to Denver, her focus is on opening her own
boutique. Wanting to cover up scars that run deeper than

her flesh, she finds in Austin a man that truly gets to her—in more ways than one.

Although wary, they embark on a slow, tempestuous burn of a relationship. When blasts from both their pasts intrude on their present, however, it will take more than a promise of what could be to keep them together.

Find out more in DELICATE INK
To make sure you're up to date on all of Carrie Ann's releases, sign up for her mailing list HERE.